Best Loved
MAGICAL
Tales for BEDTIME

Best Loved
MAGICAL
Tales for BEDTIME

SIENA

This is a Siena book

Siena is an imprint of Parragon

Parragon
13 Whiteladies Road
Clifton
Bristol BS8 1PB

Copyright © Parragon 1998

ISBN 0 75252-604-9

Printed in Great Britain

Produced by Nicola Baxter
PO Box 71
Diss Norfolk IP22 2DT

Stories by Nicola Baxter
Designed by Amanda Hawkes
Text illustrations by Duncan Gutteridge
Cover illustration by Terry Rogers

Contents

The First Little Fairy
11
The Fairy Who Couldn't Fly
25
Fairy Footprints
43
The Tooth Fairy's Problem
63
The Fairyland Fair
73
Oh, Florabell!
95

The Forest Fairy
111
The Furious Fairy
137
Fairies to the Rescue!
159
The Dew Drop Fairy
165
The Cobweb Collector
179
Your Own Special Fairy
185
The Enchanted Treasure
191
The Lost Book
215
The Flying Carpet
233

The Friendly Dragon
251

The Conjuror's Secret
271

The Christmas Pudding Wish
303

The Magic Trumpet
315

Aunt Bella's Umbrella
325

The Contrary Princess
337

Wise Wishes
349

The Apple Spell
357

Goodnight, Little Goblin
367

The Elf Who Couldn't Spell
380
The Elegant Elf
385
Mayflower's Carrots
399
The Elf in the Tree
423
Sleepy Snowdrop
439
The Goblin Gathering
453
How Petal Found a Home
469

The
First Little
Fairy

There was a time, long ago, when there were no fairies in the world. Mother Nature had no little helpers and had to do all her work by herself. As you know, fairies now help that grand old lady in many, many ways. They sprinkle dew drops on the grass in the early morning. They sweep the autumn leaves into piles that we can rustle with our feet. They mend broken spiders' webs and coax shy little flowers to open every morning.

In fact, all fairies are specially fond of flowers, and that is because the very first fairy in the world was born from a little woodland flower herself. Ever since then, fairies have almost always been given flower names.

When the world was young, Mother Nature made sure that all living things knew the part they had to play on our wonderful earth. Flowers understood that they must grow and send out buds to open beautifully in the

sunshine. Trees knew that they must grow straight and tall, stretching their branches out to shelter the little creatures living beneath them. Mother Nature taught the first birds to fly, so that they in turn could teach their own children. She showed them where to build their nests and how to hatch their eggs. She showed rabbits how to dig burrows and caterpillars how to turn into butterflies. There was no part of nature, from the tiniest ant to the largest elephant that was not guided and helped by her loving hands. And everything flourished.

When living things were in harmony, all was well, but soon life on earth began to change. Human beings ploughed up the earth and planted crops. They rooted out lovely wildflowers, calling them weeds. Instead they grew food for themselves and their animals, not thinking about the rest of nature at all.

Later on, humans built villages and towns. The smoke from their fires drifted up and sometimes hid the sun itself, which helps Mother Nature to give life to all the plants and animals on our planet. Buildings crushed the land beneath them, driving out the creatures that had lived where now streets and houses covered the earth.

As time went on, humans began to throw rubbish into the rivers, making it hard for fish to live. They chopped down trees and rooted up grasslands. Everywhere they went, they seemed to want to change Mother Nature's careful work. The poor old lady wept to see what had become of her beautiful world.

One day, Mother Nature sat in a woodland glade and buried her head in her hands in despair. There was just too much for her to do. She could not put all the ills of the world right by herself. While she was rescuing the fish from a dirty river, little animals were losing their homes as trees were destroyed. Mother Nature knew that she could not hold back the damage caused by man for ever. She felt powerless and very much alone.

On the other side of the glade, a little flower was growing. She remembered how Mother Nature had saved her only the year before. Winds had caused a huge bough to fall from the mighty tree above, crushing her beneath its weight. Mother Nature had gently lifted the branch and freed the bruised leaves of the plant. She had sprinkled her buds with sunlight and moonshine, until a few weeks later, the plant had flowered in the most beautiful way. The flower could not forget Mother Nature's kindness.

Now the old lady sat miserably in the woodland. The little flower could not bear to see her friend so very upset.

"If only I could do something to help her," said the flower to herself. "But I am only a little flower. I cannot move from this spot even to comfort Mother Nature. What a poor thing I am!"

Now it so happened that just
at that moment, a tiny amount of
stardust fell to earth. And when
stardust falls on any living thing
that is making a wish, the wish
always comes true. As the little
flower wished she could be free
to help her friend, the stardust
shimmered over her leaves and
petals. Almost at once, the flower
felt something wonderful happen.

One of her blooms began to take on a life of its own. Its yellow petals became a little dress, as delicate as gossamer. Its fragile green leaves became a tiny cloak, as light as a feather. From the centre of the flower, a beautiful little face peeped out. And most wonderful of all, the stardust itself formed two glittering wings that shimmered in the sunlight.

Without a sound, the first little fairy fluttered up into the air, flew swiftly across the clearing, and settled on Mother Nature's shoulder. She lay her little face against the old lady's worn cheek to comfort her and let her know that help was at hand. Mother Nature was no longer alone.

"I will help you all I can," said the first little fairy. Her voice was so gentle and small that the old lady could hardly hear it.

Mother Nature looked up and thought that she had seen many lovely things, but this little creature was fairer than any of them. That is why she decided to call her tiny helper a *fairy*.

"I am sure that other flowers will do what they can to help you, when they see me," said the little fairy kindly. And she was right. Soon bluebells, foxgloves, cowslips, poppies and all the other lovely flowers of the world were growing little fairies of their own, each prettier and more graceful than the last. They fluttered around Mother Nature, waiting for her to tell them what to do to help to make the world a more beautiful place.

And the wise old lady taught each fairy to help in the places she knew best, so that woodland bluebells became Bluebell Fairies, flying up to take food to mother birds who could not leave the eggs they were keeping warm. Poppy Fairies flutter into cornfields to warn the little mice who live there that the farmer is coming to cut the corn. You may have seen their little red dresses flitting through a field of golden yellow grain in summer.

As for the first little fairy, she always stays by Mother Nature's side, helping her to talk to the fairies she meets – for sometimes their voices are so tiny that the old lady cannot hear them at all – and explaining to new fairies how the wide and wonderful world of nature works.

So, if you *almost* think you see a flicker of green and yellow among the leaves, remember Mother Nature and the very first fairy.

The Fairy Who Couldn't Fly

Once upon a time, there was a Foxglove Fairy who had a darling little daughter. All babies are sweet, as they lie so trustingly in their mothers' arms, but fairy babies are even more lovable. They are very tiny, for one thing. You can put them to bed in half a walnut shell and still have plenty of room for a tiny teddy bear and a seedhead rattle.

The Foxglove Fairy called her baby daughter Little Foxglove, which is what fairies tend to do. Sometimes it is very confusing, because you may have, say, Tiny Foxglove, Little Foxglove, Medium-Sized Foxglove, Big

Foxglove and just plain Foxglove all in one family. But fairies know who is who, and that is the most important thing.

Anyway, the Little Foxglove in this story was a very contented child. She lay in her cradle and chuckled and waved her little fists. I don't know if you have ever been out in the countryside at night, but if you have, you'll know that the air is full of strange little cries. People will tell you that they are mice, and owls, and other little creatures, going about their business, but between you are me, at least some of those sounds are baby fairies! Little Foxglove, however, hardly ever cried.

"She is *such* a good baby," Foxglove told her friend Cowslip. "She is so happy all the time. Look at her now, gurgling and cooing in her cradle."

Foxglove had covered her baby's little bed in the finest gossamer and trimmed it with ribbons made of rose petals.

"She certainly is a good baby," said Cowslip, whose own child was rather a handful, "but I don't suppose it will last. All children are trouble at one time or another." (Ask your mother or father about this. Is it true?)

But Little Foxglove was soon sitting up and playing with her toys. She would wave her little fists at visitors and say "Bye Bye", which could sometimes be a little bit embarrassing if it wasn't time for them to go yet!

Still Little Foxglove was the happiest, cuddliest baby for

miles around, and Foxglove was hugely proud of her.

But one day, when she went to visit her friend Cowslip, Foxglove walked into the parlour and felt something small and soft bump into her tummy. It was Little Cowslip, and she was flying! Of course, because she had only just started, she wasn't very good at it yet, which is why she had bumped into Foxglove, but still, her little wings were carrying her up into the air, and she was getting better at fluttering and floating and flying round corners every day. She looked *so* grown up!

"How is Little Foxglove's flying coming along?" asked Cowslip, as she sat down with her friend for a cup of cornflower tea.

"Well," said Foxglove, feeling that she must tell the truth, "she hasn't really started yet. All babies learn things at different times. I expect she will make her first little flutters any day now."

But the days passed, and Little Foxglove didn't show any signs of wanting to fly. She toddled around on her fat little legs and enjoyed helping her mummy with all kinds of things, but she didn't seem interested in flapping her dear little wings.

Foxglove tried all kinds of things to tempt her daughter into the air. She carried her in her arms as she herself flew around the house and outside. She showed Little Foxglove all the interesting things there were to be seen above the ground. But the baby, although she enjoyed her little flights, didn't want to try to fly herself.

Then Foxglove tried hanging all kinds of tempting little treats from the ceiling of her home, hoping that Little Foxglove would want to fly up and grab them in her podgy little fingers. But after a visiting fairy bumped her nose on a hanging apple ring, Foxglove had to take them down again. In any case, Little Foxglove hadn't been in the least bit interested in them.

"Still not flying?" asked Cowslip, when she visited again. "Have you seen the goblin doctor?"

"Yes," replied Foxglove, wishing that her friend had not raised the subject. "He says that Little Foxglove is fine and will fly in her own good time."

Cowslip looked at the little fairy, who was watching Little Cowslip as she flitted expertly around the room. "She is rather plump," she said. "No doubt there is a lot of weight for her little wings to lift."

"Little Foxglove is cuddly, not plump," said the proud mother sharply. "She will fly in her own good time. All the fairies in my family were late flyers."

"Really?" said Cowslip. "It is quite the opposite with *us*."

Little Foxglove waved her chubby hands at Cowslip and said, "Bye Bye!" And for once her mother agreed with her!

The weeks passed, and winter turned into spring. Everywhere you looked, little creatures were building nests or making cosy homes in holes and hollows.

They were all settling down to have their babies.

Foxglove loved this time of year. She showed her little daughter a robin's nest, cleverly built in the top of an old kettle that a human had left lying about. She carried the little fairy quietly up into the branches of an apple tree to see a blackbird's nest. And she let Little Foxglove peep down a burrow under a hawthorn hedge, where a proud mummy rabbit already had eight little babies!

Little Foxglove loved to see all these little creatures. Foxglove was pleased to see how gentle her little girl was with all the living things she met.

"You are a real little fairy," she whispered, hugging her tight, "in all the ways that matter. There is plenty of time for you to learn to fly. Don't you worry. We won't listen to Cowslip."

And Little Foxglove would look up and laugh in the jolliest way imaginable, as if to say, "I'm not worried about learning to fly. It doesn't bother *me*!"

The spring days grew warmer. Soon it was that wonderful time of the year when it is not quite spring and not quite summer. The air is warm on your face, but everything is still fresh and green and new.

Foxglove took her little fairy to play in a woodland glade while she busied herself collecting eggshells. When the baby birds in their nests above hatched out, their mothers threw the empty eggshells down on to the ground below. You may find some yourself one year, but only if you are quick and look before the fairies have come around gathering, for fairies like to collect the little eggshells to make into useful things at home. They often drink their tea out of eggshell cups and eat their honeydew out of eggshell basins.

As Little Foxglove played in the mossy glade, her mother flitted here and there, putting the pretty pieces of blue, green and white eggshell that she found into a large basket. She kept Little Foxglove in sight all the time.

After a while, Little Foxglove became more interested in what was happening above her in the trees than she was in her toys on the ground. For high up on the branch of a birch tree, a real commotion was going on.

Most birds had already hatched and raised one little family. Now their babies had flown away to make homes of their own, so some birds were having another family while the evenings were still light and the sun was still warm.

High above the clearing, a mother bird had flown off to find food for her three hungry nestlings, and while she was gone, one of them, bolder than the rest, decided that he would like to try to fly. He really was being a silly little bird, for his feathers had not yet grown properly, and his little wings were not very strong. Still, some little birds don't have the sense they were hatched with, and this one was quite determined that he would hop over the edge of the nest and flutter down to the ground beneath. It didn't look very far, and he thought how proud his mother would be when she returned. Of course, if his mother had been present, she

40

would have put a stop to such experiments in no uncertain terms. Baby birds, like baby fairies, must fly when they are ready, and not a moment sooner.

As Little Foxglove looked up, the baby bird flapped his little wings and *jumped*.

It was clear a split second later that he had made a dreadful mistake. His little wings flapped uselessly, and he began to fall, down, down, towards the hard tree roots below.

But in the twinkling of an eye, there was a shimmer and a flutter, and Little Foxglove flew up and caught the little bird in her arms. Then she flew on up to the nest on the branch and gently popped the silly bird back into his cosy home with his brother and sister. Little Foxglove fluttered back down towards the ground, but because she felt happy that she had been able to help, she did a victory circuit of the whole clearing. You have never seen such beautiful flying in your life.

Standing below, Foxglove felt her eyes fill with tears as her little girl came gently to rest. Now she wasn't a baby any more, but a real little girl, and a very fine fairy indeed.

Fairy
Footprints

There was once a little girl who was very interested in fairies. More than anything else, she longed to meet a real live fairy herself. The little girl was called Emily, and she spent a lot of time looking out for clues that a fairy was nearby.

One day, Emily's mother saw her crawling along the ground with a magnifying glass in her hand, peering at the carpet.

"What *are* you doing, Emily? she asked.

"I'm looking for fairy footprints," explained the little girl. "They're very tiny, so I need a magnifying glass to see them."

"But do fairies leave footprints?" asked Emily's father, who had come in just as Emily was explaining.

"Of course they do," said Emily. *"We* leave footprints. So why shouldn't fairies?"

"Well, what if they're flying?" asked her father. "There wouldn't be any footprints then."

Emily was very quiet for a moment. She hadn't thought of that, and, of course, Daddy was perfectly right. It would be much more sensible for a fairy to fly wherever she had to go. Emily's face fell. She was never going to find a fairy footprint.

Emily's mother and father saw her disappointed little face and felt sorry for her. They wished they had let her carry on with her game without interruptions.

That night, when Mummy tucked Emily into bed, she picked up her favourite fairy story book as usual to read to her. But Emily pushed it away.

"I don't want to read about fairies any more," she said. "I'm never going to see one, so what's the point?"

Mummy tried to persuade the little girl to read her book as usual, but Emily had made up her mind. She turned over and

shut her eyes, looking most
unhappy. She didn't even say
goodnight to Mummy.

Emily's mother crept away, feeling rather upset. She felt that it was somehow her fault that her little girl was so miserable. Back in the dining room, she told her husband what had happened.

"Poor little girl," he said. "We should have left her with her dreams. Isn't there anything we can do to make her feel better?"

"Apart from finding some fairy footprints, I don't think there is," said his wife.

Emily's mother and father looked at each. Then they both grinned at the same time.

"How are we going to do it?" asked her father.

They had decided to make some pretend fairy footprints for Emily to find. Even if they weren't *real* footprints, they would make Emily happy again, and that was the most important thing. But how could they do it?

Then Mummy remembered that Emily had a tiny fairy doll with little fairy shoes.

"If we pressed one of those on an ink pad from Emily's printing kit, we could make footprints all along the windowsill," she said.

After waiting half an hour to be sure that Emily was asleep, her mummy crept into the little girl's bedroom and borrowed the fairy doll from Emily's toy cupboard. It was harder to find the ink pad from the printing kit in the dark, but she found it at last (and left inky fingerprints over the inside of the cupboard door).

Back in the dining room, Emily's mother and father practised on a piece of paper. Soon they were quite good at making fairy footprints. It was time to put their skills to good use.

This time both parents crept into the little girl's room. They carefully opened the curtains of her window. Luckily, it was a moonlit night. The moonlight shone on to the windowsill,

showing it as clearly as could be.
Very, very carefully, Daddy made
the first few footsteps.

"Watch out!" whispered
Mummy. "We mustn't leave any
smudges. That would give the
game away!"

At last there was a neat set of
footprints on the windowsill. It
looked as though a little fairy
had peeped through the curtains

at Emily, to see that she was all right. The footprints led right to the edge of the windowsill, then stopped completely.

Mummy and Daddy crept away, leaving Emily to sleep. They couldn't wait to see what happened in the morning.

Now there is a very strange thing about this story. And that is that Mummy and Daddy made the footprints because they really did not believe in fairies. They did not believe that Emily would *ever* meet a real fairy, but they wanted to make her happy by pretending that there had been one in her room.

And the even stranger thing is that there *was* a fairy in Emily's bedroom! Yes, a little fairy called Marigold lived on top of Emily's wardrobe. Her job in the little girl's home was to look after the houseplants that Mummy forgot to water and to make sure that Emily's puppy and rabbit were properly looked after.

Marigold watched as Emily's mother and father made the fairy footprints. She couldn't understand *what* they were doing. When they had left the room, she flew down from her perch and peered at the painted windowsill. How very odd! The two grown-ups had been making tiny footprints! Suddenly, the little fairy understood what they had been doing, and she was very, very angry.

Marigold took the cloth that Emily used to clean her chalkboard and wiped the fairy footprints away. How dare those grown-ups pretend that a fairy with huge feet had walked across the windowsill? Fairies pride themselves on never leaving a mess behind – not so much as a footprint, or a fingerprint, or a strand of their silky hair. Their job is to help the living things of the world, not to make messy marks themselves. Marigold sat down and wondered what to do.

First of all, she decided, she must make sure that Emily believed in fairies again. It is really important that children love fairies, for it helps the little people to do their work. Marigold crept on to Emily's bed and skipped up to where her little head lay on the pillow. Then she bent down and began to whisper in Emily's ear.

Marigold's whispering brought Emily the loveliest dream she had ever had. She dreamed she was in fairyland, talking to all her fairy friends. When she woke up in the morning, she could remember every detail of the wonderful dream.

"Now I know that there really are fairies," she said with a smile.

But a few hours before, while it was still dark, Marigold decided to teach Emily's mother and father a lesson too. She hurried into the sitting room and saw that the soot from the fire was cold but had not yet been swept up. Carefully, she dipped her dainty little feet into the soot, then she fluttered her wings and flew straight to Emily's parents' bedroom upstairs. Can you guess what that clever little fairy did then? Quite against her training and all the fairy lore, she ran lightly across the white cover on the bed, leaving little black footprints behind her. She knew that the cover could be washed, and no real harm had been done, but she wanted to teach those cheeky grown-ups that fairy footprints are a serious matter, not something to be made a joke of.

When she had finished making her footprints, Marigold flew to the bathroom and washed her dirty little shoes in soapy water. They were soon as good as new, and she hung them on the radiator to dry, intending to pick them up before morning. The little shoes were so tiny that they dried very quickly.

The next day dawned bright and clear. Emily's Mummy and Daddy woke up and had a little argument about whose turn it was to go and make the tea. In fact, whenever there was an argument, it was always because it was really Emily's father's turn. In the end, he hopped out of bed and put on his dressing gown.

Emily's father was just about to leave the room when he noticed what looked like some dirty marks on the bedcover. He bent forward to take a closer

look and let out a small whistle
of surprise.

"What is it?" asked Emily's
mother, sitting up in bed.

"What do you make of this?"
asked her husband.

"Has that puppy been on the
bed again?" cried Emily's mother.

"No, I don't think so," her
husband replied. "These marks
are much too tiny, but they are
definitely footprints."

Then both the grown-ups
remembered the trick they had
played on Emily the night before.

"She must have found the
footprints and known it was us,"
said the little girl's father. "Then

she came and made these little footprints in the same way for revenge. What a clever little girl!"

But Emily's mother was looking more closely at the marks.

"These are much smaller than the ones we made," she said, "and Emily doesn't have a doll that is smaller than her fairy doll. The only thing that could have made prints as small as these is..."

"Yes?" asked her husband.

"... is a *real* fairy!"

"Oh, that's ridiculous," cried Emily's daddy. "There are no such things as fairies. You know that, darling."

"Do I?" asked his wife. "You know, now that I've seen this, I'm not too sure."

"I'm going to settle this once and for all," said Emily's daddy, hurrying across the landing to his little girl's room. He could have sworn that everything was exactly as he and his wife had left it the night before, but the footprints on the windowsill were quite definitely gone.

"It's settled," he told his wife. "Emily woke in the night and saw the footprints on her windowsill. She realised it was us and decided to give us a taste of our own medicine. There are quite definitely no such things as fairies. Now I suggest we don't discuss it any more. Personally, I feel too silly about what we did to want to mention it to Emily."

So Emily never did know that there had been fake fairy footprints on her windowsill. She didn't know that she had a fairy living on top of her wardrobe either, although sometimes she almost thought she saw the flicker of little silver wings.

Emily's mother still wasn't sure what she thought, but her father was quite sure – until he found two tiny little slippers in the bathroom when he went to shave!

The Tooth
Fairy's
Problem

Have you ever had a visit from the tooth fairy? Perhaps you have not yet lost any of your baby teeth. When you do, you should put your old tooth under your pillow or in a little bag when you go to sleep that night. The tooth fairy will come and take away your old tooth, leaving you a little surprise in return.

Now this job, as you can imagine, keeps the tooth fairy very busy. There are lots of children all over the world, and at some time or another, every one of them loses some teeth. Then the tooth fairy has to make sure she visits them all before morning. Luckily, while one part of the world is in darkness, another part is enjoying the middle of the day, so the tooth fairy only has to concentrate on half the world at a time. But that is still an awful lot of teeth for her to collect!

Now the tooth fairy is no bigger than any of the other

fairies on earth. She finds it quite easy to carry a little baby tooth from the front of your mouth. Teeth from the back of your mouth are much bigger, so sometimes the tooth fairy has rather a struggle to carry the tooth back to fairyland.

After working very hard one week last winter, the tooth fairy felt that she could not go on any more. She went to Mother Nature and explained her problem.

"I don't know what to do," she said. "Are the children of the world getting bigger? It feels to me as though their teeth are becoming heavier and heavier. I can hardly lift them to bring them back to fairyland. After working all day, I have to visit some of the children in the other half of the world, so I hardly ever get any sleep. And with all those heavy teeth, I'm becoming very tired. In fact, I'm exhausted."

"Oh dear, that will never do," said Mother Nature. "Let me think about this, my dear, and I will give you my opinion in a little while. Come back to see me at this time tomorrow, and I will see what I can do."

"Thank you, Mother Nature," replied the tooth fairy. "I shall return tomorrow. Goodbye!"

Mother Nature thought long and hard about the difficulty, but she could not imagine how to solve it. Even if she found more fairy helpers for the tooth fairy (and it is a very specialised job that not all fairies can do), she could not do anything about the heaviness of the teeth.

After thinking for a long time, Mother Nature became tired. She decided to go for a walk to clear her head. It was very pleasant in the countryside. Old Mother Nature walked along beside a stream, seeing meadows full of flowers and trees spreading out their green leaves in the

sunshine. In fact, it was so pleasant that Mother Nature decided to sit down for a rest. In no time at all, she had fallen fast asleep on a grassy bank.

Now Mother Nature works just as hard as the tooth fairy, so it was not surprising that she felt tired in the middle of the day,

but her sleep did not last for
long. As the old lady took in a
deep breath, she felt something
tickling her nose, and she woke
up. *Atishooo!* Mother Nature
sneezed the tickle away.

But as Mother Nature was
getting to her feet, she felt
another tickle on her nose.
Looking up, she saw that the air
was full of dandelion seeds, each
floating below its own parachute
of fluffy silk. It was one of these
that had made Mother Nature
sneeze a few moments before.

As she watched the little seeds
bobbing in the air, Mother
Nature had a wonderful idea.

Next day, when the tooth fairy came to call on Mother Nature, she found the old lady hard at work. She seemed to be talking very seriously to a group of Dandelion Fairies.

"Now, my dears," she said, "you understand what you have to do? It is mainly a question of co-ordination. As long as you talk to each other and to the tooth fairy, we shall never have a problem of under- or over-supply, shall we?"

"No, Mother Nature," replied the Dandelion Fairies, bobbing little curtseys in their yellow frilly dresses.

It was not long before Mother Nature had explained to the tooth fairy that the Dandelion Fairies would attach dandelion seeds to all the large teeth. This would make them float in the air, so that they would be easier for the tooth fairy to carry.

"That's a wonderful idea!" said the tooth fairy. "You are clever, Mother Nature."

"No, no," said the old lady. "Nature is clever. I just do what I can to help."

So if, in the night after you lose one of your baby teeth, you suddenly sneeze, you will know what has been happening!

The
Fairyland
Fair

Sometimes the fairies all over the world seem to be in a flutter. If you half close your eyes when you are out in the countryside, you may see them flitting here and there, looking busier and more excited than usual. That's because it's time for the Fairyland Fair.

The Fairyland Fair is a wonderful event. All the fairies that can possibly manage it come along, and that is a lot of fairies. In fairy time, the Fair lasts for three days, but in human time, that is only about three minutes, so humans do not usually notice that all the fairies have disappeared for a little while. Since most humans never see a fairy in all their lives, very few people know about the Fairyland Fair. I thought you might like to share this fairy secret. Be careful who else you tell, won't you?

Now the Fairyland Fair is like human fairs in lots of ways, but in other ways it is very different. There are stalls and sideshows. Fairies love to play games like "Knock the poppy head off the turnip" or "Find the hidden mustard seed". There are fairground rides, too, with the dearest little swinging boats made from peanut shells and a roundabout with hanging hazlenut shells to sit in. Of course, only fairies can fit on the rides, which is one reason why only fairies are invited.

It came as a shock to the Fair Committee (chaired by Mother Nature) one year to find that several little elves had been caught disguising themselves as fairies in order to come to the Fairyland Fair. In fact, no one would have discovered this at all, if one little elf had not been found sleeping under the "Guess the weight of the acorn" stall. She had already changed back

into her elfin clothes, but her
fairy disguise was lying beside her.

Just a minute, you will say.
Elves don't look anything like
fairies! They have pointed ears
for one thing and absolutely no

wings at all. Well, that's true, but when an elf has on a sweet little fairy cap of sky-blue petals and is wearing a cloak of green velvet, it is very hard to tell that he or she is not a fairy.

You may be wondering, too, why it should matter that elves attended the Fairyland Fair. There is, I'm afraid, a history of coolness between elves and fairies. It started when elves were heard to say that fairies were *silly*. Now, like me, you have probably met a great many elves who are much, much sillier than any fairy in the world, but that is not how elves see it. Just as they have always thought that goblins are fierce and a little frightening, they have always considered fairies to be silly and not very clever. And this just goes to show how careful you must be to find out if what you hear about a person is true or just a story, for goblins are not in the least bit fierce, and fairies are some of the cleverest little people I know.

For a long time, in her early days, Mother Nature tried to be friendly with the elves. She hoped that they too might help her in her work. But elves are much more interested in their own lives and customs. They do not care for nature as fairies do. In fact, even goblins are better informed about how the world works that elves are. That is why goblins often make very good doctors, and even fairies call on them if they are ever sick or hurt. And that is about the only thing that elves and fairies have in common, for elves too use goblin doctors whenever they need them.

And what do fairies think of elves? Well, of course, no one likes to know that someone thinks they are silly and stupid. Fairies, not unnaturally, resent the unthinking views of most elves. Quite often, the elves that talk most frequently about the silliness of fairies are the very same elves that have never in their lives met one!

When she heard that elves had been visiting the Fairyland Fair, Mother Nature did not know what to do. She was a dear and friendly old lady, as you know, and she would have liked to have invented all the elves who wanted to come – and goblins too, for that matter. But Mother Nature also knew that where lots of elves are gathered together, there is often *trouble*. And the last thing that Mother Nature wanted at the wonderful Fairyland Fair was any kind of commotion or difficulty.

In view of this, a notice was put up on a tree at the outskirts of the Fair.

Fairyland Fair

Fairies only.

Elves not welcome.

By order of the Fair Committee.

Now this notice was not very friendly. It might have been better if someone had explained to the elves why they were not welcome. As it was, they took one look at the notice and declared that they wanted nothing to do with such snooty fairies. Such a notice, they said, only proved how silly fairies were, for any fair at which elves were present was bound to be superior to a fairies-only event.

Mother Nature was not very happy about the notice either, but she could not think of anything else to do. She could not bear to think of there being trouble at the Fairyland Fair.

Strangely enough, it was this very notice that ended the bad feeling between the elves and the fairies. It happened like this.

Fairies, on the whole, do what they are told by Mother Nature. They are not argumentative by nature, and they feel happiest when they are helping another living creature.

Elves, on the other hand, will argue at the drop of a hat. At the first sign of a disagreement, they will call an elfin meeting. This gathering gives everyone a chance to put forward his or her views, but the disadvantage is that the meeting can last for days. And at the end of it, the elves are very often no further forward than they were at the very beginning.

That is why, when a little elf called Berry saw the notice, he decided at once to ignore it. Berry was a nice little elf, who did his best at everything he tried, but when someone told him not to do something, his elfin nature made him want to rebel.

"I *will* go to the Fair," he said to himself, and he went at once to find a disguise.

As I said before, it is not too difficult to disguise yourself as a fairy if you wear a hat and a cloak, and that is exactly what Berry did, but he had forgotten that the cloak must be a very long one, for elfin feet are much, much larger than fairy ones.

Not realising that his feet were showing, Berry strolled through the Fair, until he came to a stall selling fresh vegetables. Elves are very fond of vegetables, especially carrots, so Berry stopped and looked at what was on display.

However, it was not long at all before Berry's attention strayed from the vegetables and fixed on the lovely young fairy who was looking after the stall. She was the most beautiful little creature that Berry had ever seen. He

listened as she spoke to her customers and soon realised that she was a very merry, clever little fairy.

A clever little fairy? Berry felt that something was wrong, somewhere. Everyone knew that fairies were silly, didn't they? But the more that Berry listened, the more he realised that fairies are just as lively and intelligent as any elf – and perhaps more so than some.

It wasn't long, either, before Berry realised that the little fairy had noticed him. She spoke kindly to him, which made Berry stammer and blush and fall over himself. The little fairy laughed, and her tinkling voice made Berry's heart turn over. He stayed by the stall all afternoon, occasionally buying vegetables so that he did not look too conspicuous.

By the end of the afternoon, the little fairy found that she liked her young visitor very well, and Berry found that he needed a wheelbarrow to take home all the vegetables he had bought!

Next morning, bright and early, Berry returned to the Fair. He was determined to ask the clever little fairy, whose name, he knew, was Primrose, if he could see her after the Fair had finished, which was the very next day.

Primrose blushed when Berry asked his question.

"I don't know," she said. "I've never had a friend who was an elf before."

"H-h-how did you know?" stammered Berry, blushing to the roots of his hair.

Primrose looked down at Berry's feet and smiled.

"Those aren't fairy feet," she said, shaking her head in fun.

The next day, Berry and Primrose did meet – and the day after that, and the day after *that*. They soon realised that they would like very much to be married, but such a thing had

never been heard of before.
Primrose decided that the best
thing would be to talk to Mother
Nature, who understood so many
things and might have an answer
to this difficult problem.

When the two young people
stood before her, Mother Nature
smiled. It was so obvious that
they were happy together. Berry
had taken off his fairy disguise, so
it was clear that he was an elf.

"How can I help you, my
dears?" asked Mother Nature,
although in fact she already
knew perfectly well.

"We should like to be married,"
said Primrose and Berry, "but we

are afraid that our families will not be happy. What shall we do?"

"Why, you must talk to them," said wise old Mother Nature. "You, Berry, must show Primrose's family what a fine, upstanding young elf you are, with good prospects and every hope of giving your wife a happy and comfortable life. You should mention that you love her too, of course. And you, Primrose, must show Berry's family that fairies are not the silly creatures they believe them to be. And you should mention that you love him, too."

"We will," said the young couple.

Well, it took a long time to convince both families, but at last they agreed that the young people could be happy. The wedding, which at first was planned to be a small affair, grew and grew, until practically everyone in Elftown and all the local fairies were invited. It was a wonderful party!

Nowadays, fairies and elves all remember that it was at the wedding of Berry and Primrose that they first really saw each other without listening to a lot of silly stories and prejudices. That fairies are clever and elves are kind became clear for all to see.

Nowadays, so many elves and fairies have set up home together that it is no longer wondered at.

Berry and Primrose are very happy together. They have three little children who share all the best features of elves *and* fairies. And each year, the whole family goes to the Fairyland Fair.

The notice outside has changed.

Fairyland Fair

Everyone welcome.

By order of the Fair Committee.

Oh,
Florabell!

Everyone knows that fairies are fragile, graceful little creatures. Well, almost all of them are. But there was once a fairy called Florabell who liked cakes. It didn't much matter what kind of cakes they were. Sponge cakes, buns, cherry cakes and chocolate cakes were all favourites. It didn't help that Florabell's mother was an excellent cook, who loved to fill her cake tins with blueberry muffins and caramel slices.

Florabell loved to empty those cake tins as fast as her mother filled them, which was often more than once a day!

I expect you can guess what happens to a fairy who munches cakes all day. Yes, she becomes a well-rounded fairy. Then, if she carries on eating cakes, she becomes a plump fairy. More cakes make her a chubby fairy. Another swiss roll or two and she is a podgy fairy. A couple more visits to the cake tins and there is no doubt about it. That fairy is a fat fairy, and hardly anyone wants to be that.

At the time of this story, Florabell was a chubby, or maybe slightly podgy fairy. She didn't like having to have her dresses let out, but she liked cakes a lot more than she disliked going to the dressmaker. It was no contest really.

At first, Florabell's mother was not at all concerned about her daughter. She liked plump babies and she thought that toddlers really should be cuddly. Florabell seemed to be happy and learning fast. But by the time she was ready to go to school, Florabell was quite a large girl, and her flying was not as good as it should be. That wasn't really surprising. Fairies' wings are delicate little things, meant to lift a fragile fairy from the ground. They were never designed for hoisting hefty girls into orbit.

At last the day came when Florabell's mother took her to the goblin doctor.

"I really can't think why she is *quite* so cuddly," she said.

"I can," said the doctor. "She eats too many sweet things. Why, I saw her munching biscuits in the waiting room."

"She was *hungry*," said Florabell's mother. "A growing girl needs energy."

"Nonsense!" said the doctor. (Goblin doctors are not known for their bedside manners.) "Your daughter needs fresh air, exercise and good food. She does *not* need cakes, or biscuits, or buns. She would not come to any harm if one of those sickly sweet things never passed her lips again. Indeed, she might be a great deal better. And think about her teeth! All those sweet things will do *them* no good at all either. I'm afraid that Florabell must rely on *you* to set a good example as her mother."

Florabell's mother heard this with a sinking heart. She rather enjoyed cakes, and biscuits, and buns too. But she had her daughter's best interests at heart, so when she got home, she put her bakery books well out of reach at the top of the bookshelf and began preparing healthy salads instead.

Over the next few weeks, Florabell's mother got quite a bit thinner. She felt a good deal healthier, too, and would have been able to run energetically about after her little daughter if only that daughter had been running! For Florabell looked exactly the same, or even slightly, well, *chubbier*.

Florabell's mother racked her brains to think of what was going wrong. She was very sure that Florabell was not eating cakes, or biscuits, or buns at home. The teacher at the school assured her that Florabell was not eating naughty things there either.

Florabell's mother was forced to turn detective. For one whole week she kept track of where her little girl went and who she saw. By the end of the week, the poor mother knew where the problem lay – it was Granny.

Florabell's mother went round to see *her* mother straight away. She expected the visit to be difficult, for the old lady enjoyed baking as much as she did.

"Florabell seems to be spending a lot of time with you now," the little girl's mother began.

"Oh yes," said Granny. "It's lovely. She always calls in after school. Poor wee mite, she's so hungry after a busy afternoon that she can't make that long journey home unless she has a little snack here. I often give her something to put in her lunchbox for the next day as well. I don't want to criticise, dear, but a child can't live on tomatoes alone. She's not very fond of salad."

Florabell's mother restrained herself with difficulty. All these weeks of lettuce, and it seemed that the only person who had been eating it was herself!

"You're looking a little peaky, dear," said her mother. "I don't think you're eating properly. Let me get you a nice slice of cake and some hot chocolate. Florabell loves that."

"No, thank you, Mother," said Florabell's mummy, and she proceeded to explain to the old lady exactly why it was important not to give Florabell the sweet things she obviously loved so much.

It took quite a lot of explaining before Granny got the message. She loved her granddaughter so much that she found it difficult to think of her as anything but completely perfect.

Florabell's mummy had to smile when she looked at her own mother. The old lady loved cakes as much as anyone, but she was much slimmer and more active even than her daughter.

"I know *you* seem to be able to eat anything and never put on an ounce of weight," said Florabell's mother, "but the rest of us aren't like that. We have to be much more careful about what we eat."

"Well, I try to keep active," said her mother with a smile. "Our little Florabell should do more running about."

"When?" asked her daughter. "The children laugh at her during sports lessons at school."

"Well, after school then," said Florabell's granny.

"After school she's *here*," said Florabell's mummy, "filling her little tummy with sweet things."

"You're right," said the old lady at last. "I've been trying to be kind to my little darling, but instead I've been causing her harm. You just leave it to me. I'll put things right, I promise."

Over the next few weeks, Florabell continued to go to Granny's house after school, but she didn't get any plumper. In fact, she began to look a little bit thinner, and she had a pinkness in her cheeks and a brightness in her eyes that had never been there before.

"You don't have to go to Granny's house *every* night," said her mother gently one evening, as she tucked her little daughter into bed.

"Oh yes, I do," said Florabell, "poor Granny needs me."

"Does she?" asked her mother, thinking of the lively and happy old lady she knew and loved. "Why is that exactly, darling?"

"Well, she has a terrible urge to eat sweet, sticky things that are bad for her teeth and, at her age, almost every part of her," said Florabell seriously. "She needs me to be there to stop her doing it. I've had to be careful not to eat things like that in front of her, so that I don't upset her."

"Have you?" asked her mother with a smile. "That's very kind of you. But don't you miss those things yourself?"

"Not if it's for Granny's sake," said the little girl firmly. "I'd do anything in the world for her."

There was no doubt about it, Florabell was soon beginning to look not so much chubby as plump. And pretty soon after that, she began to seem not so much plump as well-rounded.

Florabell seemed to have so much more energy now, too. One day, her mother found her practising skipping in the garden.

"That's very good, darling," she said. "I didn't know you could skip so well."

"Oh," said Florabell, "I have to, for Granny, you know."

"Really?" asked her mother.

"Oh, yes. The doctor has told Granny that she must skip for

half an hour a day. She finds it *so* hard to do, poor old thing. I have to practise really hard so that I can show her how. Then I do her exercises with her to make sure she does them properly. You know, if I'm not there every minute, she just stops. Isn't that silly? Everyone knows it's important to do exercise, don't they."

"Yes," said Mummy with a smile. "You're quite right."

"Which reminds me," said her slim little girl. "you need to skip too. You never do any exercise."

"Oh, Florabell!" laughed her mummy. "Oh, Mother!"

The Forest
Fairy

When you ask someone what they know about fairies, they often talk about the way that they are small and pretty. They will probably mention the fact that they have gauzy little wings and can fly. And last of all, they will mention the fact that they have fairy wands. You know the kind of thing – a little stick with a star on top.

Now the fact is that most fairies don't have wands at all. When they are flying about in the countryside, they really need both hands free to help other living things. Most of the time, a wand would get in the way.

So where have we got this wand idea from? Well, not many people have seen fairies, as you know. You may have been one of the lucky ones. A long time ago, someone saw a little fairy carrying a fallen star back to its place in the sky. Young stars sometimes do slip. They need to be put gently back in place, using a special star stick.

I can see that you need me to explain about star sticks, too. The fact is, although stars can look cold and glittery in the sky, in fact they are rather hot. In order not to burn their little fingers, fairies pick them up on the end of a stick, called a star stick. That way, they can pop them back into the sky without any problem.

You can imagine what happened. The human being long ago caught sight of a fairy just as she was flying up to put the star back. He didn't know about star sticks, so he assumed that what she was carrying was a magic wand. He was so excited about what he saw that he told lots and lots of other people. And that is how the story about fairy wands was spread.

Now it is a funny thing about rumours. Sometimes they spread so far and so fast that they almost become true, especially if they get back to the person they are about.

After the silly human had seen what he thought was a fairy wand, one of the people he told was a friend of his, who was a painter. Before you could say "Stardust nonsense," the painter had made a portrait of the fairy his friend had described, and, of course, she was carrying a fairy wand. This picture became quite famous, but still, it would not have been seen by very many people, if some bright spark had not decided to print a small version of it on to the postage stamps of a large country. They looked so pretty that other countries copied the idea, and soon there was hardly anyone in the whole world who had not seen the picture of the fairy with her star stick – or fairy wand as they thought.

In case you are interested, this is what the picture looked like:

Now I'm sure you will agree
with me that the picture does
not look like any of the fairies we
have seen. But most of the
people who saw the stamp had
no idea what a fairy should look
like. They thought it was a lovely
picture and left it at that.

But the trouble is that human
beings always leave an incredible
amount of rubbish lying about.
Fairies are constantly clearing up
what people leave behind, and
some of the things they throw
away so carelessly are used
envelopes. That is how several
fairies saw the famous stamps
and the picture of the fairy

carrying a star stick and a fallen star.

Now you may remember me telling you that each kind of fairy has a special job to do. Moonflower Fairies keep the moon bright and polished, so that it shines down on us each night. If they didn't, that old moon would get terribly dusty, sitting up in the sky. Sunflower Fairies make sure that the faces of even the shyest little flowers are turned towards the sun each morning. Of course, it is Starflower Fairies that put the stars back in the sky when they have fallen to earth by mistake.

A fairy who works in deserts
or woodlands or rivers may
never have met a Starflower
Fairy, just as they are not likely
to have met a Tigerlily Fairy
(who has a very dangerous job
concerning tigers, which I will
not go into here). So when these
other fairies saw the human
postage stamp with the picture
of a fairy on it, even they
thought she might be carrying a
magic wand. That is the way that
silly stories are spread.

"I wish I could have a magic
wand," said one little fairy to her
mother one day. "It would look
just right with my new dress."

"Well, I haven't got one, Briar Rose," her mother said, "and I don't know any other fairy who has. I think they must be some kind of special thing that only fairies in pictures have. I've met a lot of fairies in my time, and not one of them has had a fairy wand."

Briar Rose always believed what her mother said, of course, but she believed the evidence of her own eyes, too. She knew what she had seen on the postage stamp, and she still thought that the fairy wand looked very pretty. If there were wands to be had, she wanted one. And she wanted it badly.

Week after week, Briar Rose saved up her pocket money. She did not know how much a fairy wand would cost, but she made a sensible guess. When she thought she had enough, she went along to the general store in Goblinville.

Now goblins, as well as being very good doctors, are also excellent shopkeepers. They are sensible about money and clever enough to keep a track of what they have in stock so that they never (well, hardly ever) run out.

The goblin who kept the general store in Goblinville smiled at Briar Rose when she came into the shop with a serious expression on her pretty face. It showed she meant business.

"What can I do for you, young lady?" he asked.

"Please," said Briar Rose, holding out her pocket money, "I'd like to buy a fairy wand."

"A fairy wand?" said the goblin. "I'm afraid we don't have any call for those. You are the first fairy ever to ask me for one. I'm quite sure that I don't have one in stock at the moment, but if you would be kind enough to wait just a moment, I will get my big catalogue and see if I could send away for one for you. It would only take a day or two."

So the goblin went into the back of his shop and came back with a huge, dusty book. It was so large that he was staggering as he carried it back to his counter and set it down.

"Now, let's have a look," he muttered, leafing through the pages. "*D* for dragons, *E* for elves, aha! Here's *F* for fairies."

The little fairy held her breath. She looked down at the money clutched in her little hand and wondered how expensive a fairy wand would be.

"*Fairy dresses, fairy furniture fairy hats, fairy pots and pans, fairy stockings, fairy wings …*

hmm, nothing here about fairy wands, I'm afraid."

But Briar Rose's attention had been caught by another item in the catalogue.

"*Fairy wings*?" she asked. "You can't buy fairy wings, can you?"

"No, no," laughed the goblin, "when I saw that it wasn't about wands, I stopped reading. That entry is for *fairy wings, special non-drying soap for*."

"*Special non-drying soap for* doesn't make sense," said Briar Rose with a puzzled look.

"I'm sorry," smiled the goblin, looking down kindly at the little fairy. "I'm not explaining very well. The catalogue puts the most important part of the item first, even if it isn't the first part. The entry should read: *Special non-drying soap for fairy wings*."

"Do I need that?" asked Briar Rose, trying to look over her shoulder at her own little wings.

"No, no," said the goblin. "I only sell that to older fairies, whose wings have become a little wrinkly, you know. Your own wings are quite beautiful as they are. Now, about this fairy wand…"

Briar Rose remembered why she had come to the shop, and that there had been no mention of a fairy wand in the catalogue.

"Could it be under something else?" she asked, now that she understood how the catalogue worked. "Like *wand, fairy* or *wand, magic*."

"I see you're getting the idea," smiled the goblin. "Let's have a look, shall we?"

But although they looked at lots of different entries, there was no mention of fairy wands in the catalogue at all.

"As I said," the goblin advised, "it's not something I've ever been asked for before. Are you sure there are such things?"

Then Briar Rose explained about the postage stamp she had

seen on a human letter. She
described it in every detail.

"Well," said the goblin. "I'm not
sure I would rely on anything that
a human being paints. They're
not very clever. I happen to know
that they have the most
extraordinarily silly ideas about
goblins. If the fairy wand is as
simple as you say, why don't you
make your own?"

"Could I?" asked Briar Rose.

"Well, I think so," said the
goblin. "It doesn't sound very
difficult to me. I can give you a
stick and some glue. All you have
to do is to find a star. I'm afraid
we don't sell those either."

He really was a very kind goblin. When Briar Rose stretched out her little hand to give him her pocket money, he shook his head.

"No, no," he said. "The stick and the glue are free. You might need your pocket money on your star-finding adventures. Good luck, little fairy!"

Clutching her stick and the glue, the little fairy hurried off to tell her mother what had happened. But her mother was out stroking pine needles with her gentle fingers, so that they all lay in one direction, not standing up on end like a hedgehog!

Briar Rose left the stick and the glue in a safe place and set off to find a star. The only thing she really knew about stars was that they were found in the sky. (She'd never heard, you see, of falling stars or the fairies who rescue them.) With her little nose in the air, Briar Rose set off in search of a shining star.

You and I, being wiser and older than Briar Rose, will know that she was not very likely to find a star in the daytime. You need a dark, clear night to see stars at their best. But Briar Rose didn't know that. She searched the skies until it was almost dark,

but she could not find a single shining star.

Then, just as the sun was going down, and the sky was taking on a lovely deep blue colour, the little fairy saw something shining in the distance. She hurried towards it, quite forgetting to notice where she was.

At last she came to the very edge of the forest. One tree stood by itself, a little way from the others. As the little fairy watched, she was astonished and delighted to see something twinkling on top of the tree. She moved closer, hardly daring to breathe. It was! It was! At the top of the tree was a little shining star, perfect for a fairy wand!

Briar Rose was so excited, she didn't think about anything else. Although it was getting dark now, she was determined not to go home until she had got her star.

Using all her strength, the little fairy flew up, up, up into the air. It was farther than she had ever flown before, but at last, just when she felt that her little wings wouldn't flutter any more, she reached the top of the tree.

But the star wasn't there. The little fairy looked up. There was the star, shining so far above her that the little fairy gave a sigh of disappointment. It had only looked as if the star was sitting on top of the tree. Now she realised that it was high above it, right up in the clear night sky. Briar Rose knew that she would never, never be able to fly so far.

Feeling sad and disappointed, the little fairy flew down to the ground. It was time to go home.

But oh dear, it was properly dark now, and each tree looked the same as its neighbour. For the first time, Briar Rose felt a little worried. No one knew where she was. They could not come to rescue her. What if she had to stay here, in the cold and dark, until morning? The thought made the little fairy shiver and shake.

As she sat under the single tree, Briar Rose heard the little squeaks and cries of the forest night. Her mother had explained to her that these were nothing to be frightened of, but it was different, somehow, when they were so near and she was on her own. Now, more than anything, Briar Rose wished her mummy, with her warm, comforting arms, was nearby.

Just then, a voice floated through the trees.

"Briar Rose! Briar Rose! Where are you?"

It *was* her mummy! In no time at all, the little fairy was safe.

"How did you find me?" she asked her relieved mother.

Then Mummy explained that she had gone to the goblin shop and heard all about the fairy wand.

"When we get home," she said, "I will make you a star from silver paper to put on the end of your wand. It will only be pretend, but I'm afraid that the picture on the stamp is only pretend too."

"That will be lovely," said Briar Rose. "My wand will be magic because *you* made it. It doesn't need a real star."

And, you know, she was right!

The
Furious
Fairy

Now some of the stories that are told in books are true, and some of them are not. This one was told to me by a very old lady, who claimed to have had many fairy friends when she was young. You will have to make up your own mind about whether you believe it or not.

Once upon a time, there were twelve good fairies who lived in a certain kingdom. One day, they were invited to the baptism of the baby daughter of the King and Queen of the kingdom. They were happy to go and give the little Princess all the blessings within their power.

Unfortunately, the King and Queen had completely forgotten to invite the thirteenth fairy, who was very old and lived in a cave in the mountains.

They had not heard from her for several years, so they thought she might have moved away.

But the thirteenth fairy heard about the Princess's birth and the party that was to be held to celebrate her baptism. And she was absolutely *furious*!

Now, you are probably thinking that this story sounds rather familiar. Doesn't the thirteenth fairy come and curse the little Princess, so that she pricks her

finger on a spindle and falls
asleep for a hundred years?

Well, I have read the story you
are thinking of in many books,
and that is exactly what happens,
but it is not the story I want to
tell you here. This story is not
about the Princess at all. It is
about what happened to the
thirteenth fairy when she went
back to her mountain home.

Have you ever done anything naughty? Really naughty? No? Are you sure? Well, if you have ever done something just a little bit naughty, you will know that you can have a rather funny feeling afterwards.

It's a feeling that makes you think maybe there's something squiggling in your tummy. And there's a funny feeling in your head as well. It's as though the only thing you can think about is that silly, naughty thing you did. I'm afraid there is only one cure for a feeling like that. You have to go and say sorry for the naughty thing, and if possible, you must

put right everything that has
gone wrong. Then, if the people
involved are kind to you and
understand that you will never,
ever do the naughty thing again,
they will smile and say you are
forgiven, and you will feel much,
much better, with no more
squiggly feelings.

Now, you can imagine, that if
you have squiggly feelings after
you have done a very little
naughty thing, you must have
really bad wriggly, jiggly, squiggly
feelings after you have done a
very bad thing. That is what
happened to the thirteenth fairy,
as you will hear.

After she had cursed the baby Princess and crashed the palace doors shut behind her, the thirteenth fairy flew away from the castle as fast as her wings would carry her. Normally, the guards in the palace would have stopped anyone who came to do harm to the King and Queen and their little one. But the guests and servants in the palace were all so shocked by what had happened that they could not move for several minutes. Then they were busy making sure that they baby was all right. It was only about five minutes later that guards came rushing out to find the

thirteenth fairy, and by then she was far, far away, flying over the mountains towards her cave.

But, if the truth be told, the furious fairy was not flying very well. Those jiggly, wriggly, squiggly feelings had been joined by a wiggly feeling in her tummy. It is hard to fly with all that going on inside you, as you can imagine. And perhaps that is why the furious fairy didn't make it back to her cave. She took her attention away from what she was doing for just a second too long and crash-landed in the middle of a wood. *Woosh! Wallop! Woomph!* And she was down.

Fairies are usually excellent flyers. Their safety record is second to none, as they are sensible enough not to fly into windows, as birds sometimes do, or try to do difficult low-flying manoeuvres when it is foggy. For this reason, fairies are not trained what to do in the event of an aerial accident. The furious fairy lay in the bush where she had fallen with no idea what to do next. She did not think that she was badly hurt, but she could not be sure.

It was then that she saw the bear! It was a big, brown, furry bear, and it was heading straight towards her, making a little growling noise as it came.

Now most bears are much more frightened of humans than humans are of them. But fairies are different. Bears *like* fairies, as they rely on them to tell them when to wake up after their long winter's sleep. In the old days, when bears decided for themselves when to go outside in search of food, they made some dreadful mistakes. One warm day was enough to wake them, but it might be in the middle of winter! A bear often wandered away from his cave in search of food only to find that the next day the snow was falling thick and fast so that he couldn't find his way home again. Since fairies took over the job, things have been much better. You hardly ever see a bear until the snow has started to melt and spring is well and truly on the way.

However, the furious fairy had no experience of bears. All she felt when she saw one coming towards her was that the squiggly, wriggly feeling had come back with a vengeance. She tried to sit up so that she could escape, but somehow she felt very wobbly, which is not surprising after a fall.

The bear came closer and closer to the furious fairy, until she could feel his hot breath on her face.

"Hmmm," said the bear. "What have we here?"

The furious fairy was so astonished to hear the bear talking her language that she forgot to be frightened for a moment. In fact, the bear was talking Bear, but fairies are very good at understanding all kinds of languages. The furious fairy had been such a bad-tempered unpleasant old fairy for so long that she had not even tried to communicate with other living things. She had completely forgotten that her old fairy skills were just rusty.

The furious fairy felt that it would be a good idea to reply to the bear.

"I've had an accident," she said, in an every softer voice than fairies usually use.

Luckily, bears always have excellent hearing.

"I can see that," said the bear. "Can I help at all?"

"I don't think so," said the thirteenth fairy, amazed that another creature should be so kind to her. "I don't think I've broken anything. It's just that the fall took my breath away, and it hasn't all come back yet."

Without another word, the bear picked her up in his strong, furry arms and turned towards a winding forest path.

"Hey! Just a minute!" called the fairy. "Where are you taking me?"

"I'm taking you back to my cave," said the bear. "You're very thin and you've had a big shock. I'll look after you until you feel well enough to fly home."

The furious fairy was about to protest, but really, she didn't feel too energetic at the moment, and the idea of something to eat was very appealing. She realised that she had not had a proper meal since she heard about the baby Princess's baptism and realised that she had not been invited. The news had made a hard, cold lump in her tummy that made it difficult to eat.

They soon arrived at the bear's cave. The fairy looked round with pleasure. She was used to caves, for she lived in one herself, and this one was very fine. The bear had a lovely soft bed and a little ledge where he ate his food. It was very cosy.

And a snack of fruit and nuts was most welcome too. The fairy ate ravenously.

When she had finished, she felt warm and full, so when the bear asked her why she had not eaten recently, she told him all about the non-existent invitation to the Princess's baptism and how it had made her feel cold and unwanted and cross.

"So what did you do about it?" asked the bear. "Did you get in touch with the palace and point out that they had made a mistake, so that they could put it right?"

"No," said the fairy.

"Did you send a present anyway, to show that there were no hard feelings?"

"No," said the fairy.

"So you just felt upset for a while but did nothing?"

"No," said the fairy. She could feel the squiggly, wriggly, jiggly feelings in her tummy again, and they were worse than ever.

Very slowly, not looking at him, the fairy told the bear what she had done.

When she looked up, the bear was shaking his big brown head.

"Oh dear," he said. "Oh dear. Oh dear. Oh dear. That's bad. That's very bad."

"I know," said the fairy. "But what's done is done. I shouldn't have got so cross, perhaps, but those other fairies were all being so goody-goody. It made me mad down to my boots."

"So what are you going to do now?" asked the bear.

"Do? Well, I'm going to go home to my cave and carry on as usual," said the fairy, but even as she said it, she knew that she would have to do more than that.

"I don't think that will take away your squiggly, wiggly feeling," said the bear seriously.

"How do you know about *that*?" cried the fairy in surprise.

"Don't you know what that feeling is?" asked the bear. "It's your conscience. It's telling you that you must put what you did right, or you will never feel really happy again."

"Is it?" asked the fairy. She dimly remembered her old mother saying something similar, many, many years ago. How very strange. She knew in her heart of hearts that the bear was right.

It was a few days before the furious fairy was ready to travel.

"Come back and see me when everything is sorted out!" called the bear, as he waved goodbye to the thirteenth fairy.

Very sensibly, the fairy put on a disguise to return to the palace. She found that everyone was still talking about what had happened at the baptism, and she heard too of the way in which the twelfth fairy had softened her curse.

"Thank goodness," said the thirteenth fairy. "That is just what I would have done myself. Now I must wait until I can break the spell for ever."

Years passed. The thirteenth fairy went about her business as usual, but now she took a special interest in the woodland creatures who lived around her cave. She was a much nicer fairy now.

At last the fairy had news from a passing bird that the whole royal palace had fallen into a deep sleep.

"No harm can come to them while they are sleeping," she said, and settled down to wait again.

Ninety-nine years later, the fairy was off on her travels again. She flew to a distant country, where a fine young prince was living. One night, the fairy crept into his room and whispered in his ear. In the morning, the Prince suddenly announced that he wanted to go travelling. The rest of the story, I think you know.

And the furious fairy? She and her friend the bear attend every royal function, including a recent wedding that I hear was very special indeed.

Fairies to
the
Rescue!

What do you do if a kitten gets stuck in a tree? Well, you stand at the bottom and call him. You hold up his bowl of kitty food and try to tempt him down. You try being cross and you try being nice. You may even point out the nice strong branch that he should jump on to. But the chances are that none of these ideas will work. Kittens, once they get stuck, seem to get well and truly stuck. And somehow, they can't remember exactly how they managed to climb up to where they are now. If only they could remember where they had put each little paw. Coming down would be so much easier. But kittens are not as sensible as fairies. They prefer just to sit in the tree and wait to be rescued.

When all other ideas have been tried, most people call the fire brigade. These fine people are usually only too happy to help, as long as they are not busy fighting a fire, of course.

Along comes the fire engine. When it gets very near, it flashes its lights to amuse the children. Then the engine parks safely by the side of the road, and the firefighters get out.

"Where's the little rascal?" they ask, peering up into the tree.

And there he is, sitting on his branch, looking pathetically down at the ground.

"No problem" say the brave firefighters. "We'll have him down in no time."

Up go the long, long ladders, and up go the firefighters. Nearer and nearer to the little kitten they come until ... have they got him? Yes ... no ... yes ...oh! *Just* before the first firefighter reaches the kitten, he jumps down from his branch and runs merrily down the tree into your arms!

Ask any firefighter and he or she will tell you that happens all the time.

Now most people believe that the reason for the kitten's annoying behaviour is that it just doesn't want to be caught. When the firefighter comes near, its fear vanishes and it skips down the tree to avoid those reaching hands.

But what really happens is very different. Shall I let you into a secret? Don't tell, will you?

It is fairies who are to blame!
Yes, fairies, who are normally
such good and kind little
creatures, just occasionally like to
have a joke.

They flutter up into the tree
with the kitten and say, "Stay
where you are until we say the
word. This is a good game, isn't
it?" And the kitten is only too
happy to play along.

So next time you see a kitten
apparently trapped in a tree, look
very carefully at the leaves and
branches nearby. You just might
see a cheeky little face peeping
out at you, if you look hard enough!

The Dew Drop Fairy

Have you ever been out in the early morning, before the sun has had a chance to dry the grass? You will find that every little blade of green has a sparkling dew drop on its tip. It looks so pretty if the sunlight makes the dew drops twinkle, and it's the Dew Drop Fairy that we have to thank for it.

The Dew Drop Fairy is always up and about before the sun has risen, and she has gone back to the shelter of her little toadstool home by the time the sun is high in the sky. She has spent so long among dew drops that she fears she would melt away as they do if

she had to sit in the hot sun.

One day, the Dew Drop Fairy
received a letter written on a leaf.
That is how fairies usually send
their messages, and they give
them to little birds who are flying
in the right direction for delivery.

This leaf had come a very, very
long way. It was from the Dew
Drop Fairy's cousin in the
rainforests of South America.

I don't know if you have ever read about the rainforest. It is a wonderful place, where thousands and thousands of plants and animals make their homes. In fact, there are probably hundreds of kinds of insect that human beings have never seen, although fairies, of course, know them well.

The Dew Drop Fairy's cousin was called the Pitcher Plant Fairy. She had a special job to do. In the rainforest there are curious plants that live high up in the trees. Their roots do not reach down to the ground but are lodged in the bark of the trees on whose branches they perch. They take some of the food they need from the trees, and the trees don't seem to mind.

Now the curious thing about these plants is that they have a little basin in the middle. Where the petals meet at the centre, there is a hollow part, which fills up with water. It is the Pitcher Plant Fairy's job to make sure that the pitcher plant is always full of water. You are probably wondering why this matters, but the fact is that lots of little insects and animals rely on their treetop basin for water. Some little frogs even sit in the pitcher plant's pool all day, high up in the trees! They never come down to splash in an ordinary pool.

The Pitcher Plant Fairy told her cousin about the wonderful rainforest in her letter, and she finished up with even more exciting news.

"The rains are coming," she said, "so my work is not needed for a while. I am coming to visit you by the next available seabird."

The Dew Drop Fairy was terribly excited. She hurried about, making sure that her house was neat and tidy and her spare bed was made up with thistledown pillows and a blanket of sheep's wool, gleaned from the hedges and fences where the sheep leave it.

The Dew Drop Fairy wasn't sure when exactly her cousin was coming, but she kept a sharp look out whenever any large birds flew overhead. At last, one sunny morning, she heard a squawk outside and rushed out to find her cousin saying goodbye to a black-headed gull.

"Thank you so much for bringing me," said the fairy.

"Don't mention it," replied the bird. "I was glad of the company."

Well, the Dew Drop Fairy was glad of the company too. She

hurried her cousin into the house and begged her to sit down to rest after her long journey.

"Oh, we never rest in the rainforest," said her cousin, who was wearing a bright red and green and blue costume. "We are on the go all the time," she went on. "There's something about the steamy heat of the forest that is very invigorating."

"Oh, I shouldn't like that at all," said the Dew Drop Fairy. "I don't like to go out in the sunshine, for fear that I would melt away like my own dew drops."

"That's nonsense, surely," said her cousin briskly. "Fairies don't melt away. They're much too well made for that."

The Pitcher Plant Fairy looked critically at her cousin.

"You look so pale," she said, "almost like a ghost, but it's not surprising if you never go out into the sunshine. If there's one thing I'll do while I'm here, it's to introduce you to a little light and warmth. Just look at your grey-green clothes. How dull they are."

"I couldn't wear bright colours like yours in my job," said the Dew Drop Fairy. "Why, human beings out for an early morning walk with their dogs would spot me easily on the green grass. And that would be the end of me, I can assure you."

"Really?" asked the Pitcher Plant Fairy. "Are humans in your world so dangerous? In the rainforest, the Indians love to catch sight of us among the leaves. They would never dream of doing us harm. My clothes are bright to fit in with the other rainforest creatures. You should see the parrots with their brilliant feathers! They are much more beautiful than anything you have here. Look, I've brought some little pictures for you to see."

The Dew Drop Fairy looked curiously at the pictures of

parrots and colourful frogs. There were flowers too, in bright, hot colours. They made the flowers that the Dew Drop Fairy was used to look rather dull and drab.

At first, the Dew Drop Fairy was happy to hear stories of the amazing place where her cousin lived, but before long she began to be tired of it. It all sounded so bright and vivid, she felt that her own tender senses would never stand it.

"Come back with me," begged her cousin. "It's only fair. I've seen where you live. Now you must come and visit me. I can tell just by looking at you that you don't get out much. A change will do you all the good in the world.

"Let me think about it," said the Dew Drop Fairy.

Next morning, while her visitor was still in bed, the Dew Drop Fairy went out to sprinkle dew drops as usual. She soon finished her work and stopped to look over the gentle countryside.

"It's lovely, isn't it?" said Mother Nature, coming up behind her. "Of course, I love all the living things in the world, but this lovely scene, with its gentle colours, is one of my favourites. And I love the sharp scent of autumn in the air. You know, in some places, they have no seasons. It is the same all year round. I prefer our changing scene."

"So do I," said the fairy.

So the Dew Drop Fairy didn't go to South America, although she does now sometimes venture into the sunshine. "I live in the loveliest place on earth," she says. "Just as my cousin does!"

The Cobweb Collector

Once upon a time, there was a little fairy who loved to collect cobwebs. It wasn't part of her usual job, but she found them so useful, she could never have enough of them. From the lacy cobwebs, the little fairy made all kinds of beautiful things. She knitted them into shawls and wove them into hammocks. She used the threads to tie up little parcels and to moor her oak-leaf boat to the bank. She really did not know what she would do without cobwebs. Eventually, although it was not her real name, everyone called her the Cobweb Fairy.

Now there was only one creature who loved cobwebs more than the little fairy I have described, and that was the spider who spun them! He liked to spin several webs in different places. Then he would go round and visit them in turn to see if he had caught any flies. You can imagine his annoyance when he found on a regular basis that several of his favourite cobwebs were missing!

The spider understood that cobwebs are fragile things, and accidents will happen. He knew that sometimes the wind would blow them away, and occasionally a bird will fly into one or a passing human thoughtlessly brush it down. But all those events leave little threads behind to wave in the air. Someone, the spider realised, was snipping his cobwebs neatly through and collecting them on purpose.

There was only one thing to do. The spider lay in wait by one of his webs. As soon as the Cobweb Fairy arrived with her little scissors, he darted out and wrapped her tightly in one of his sticky threads.

"What do you mean by stealing my precious cobwebs?" he asked.

"I'm sorry," said the fairy.

"Do you usually steal things?"
asked the spider.

"No, no. I didn't think I was
stealing. I thought the webs were
abandoned. You weren't here,
after all. How was I to know?"

The spider could tell that she
was telling the truth. And she had
a fair point. He didn't in the least
mind if she took his old webs.

"We'll have to think of a sort of
signal," he said.

So now, when the spider is ready
to abandon a web, he weaves a
special pattern in it to tell the
Cobweb Fairy. Look very carefully
at cobwebs – but don't touch
them – and you may see it, too!

Your Own
Special
Fairy

Did you know that you have your own special fairy? It's true. There is a little fairy whose job it is just to look after you. She tries hard to keep you safe and to make sure that you are happy, but sometimes that is not an easy job. Children often make it difficult for their own special fairies to do their best.

For one thing, it is very important that you believe in your fairy. No fairy can work well if she thinks that people are not taking her seriously. The best way to let your fairy know that you appreciate everything she is doing for you is to think about her from time to time. Your fairy can read your thoughts (although other fairies cannot), and she will glow with pride to know that you are wishing her well.

If you shut your eyes now, and sit very still, and think about your fairy and how you imagine she looks, you may just feel her settling ever so gently on your shoulder. If you open your eyes, she will fly away so quickly that you will only just see a fluttering and a movement out of the corner of your eye.

So what does your fairy look like? I can tell you, even though I don't know what *you* look like!

She has hair of ... your colour! She has eyes of ... your colour! Her skin is like yours and so is her smile. Can you see her a little more clearly now?

When you are ill, your fairy is very sad, but she never leaves your side. Even in the middle of the night, she sits by your head, stroking your hair so gently that you cannot even feel it.

When you are naughty, your fairy is sad too. She begins to feel faint and ill, wondering if you will be good again to make her feel better. For fairies do not like other people to be unhappy, and sooner or later you being naughty

will make someone else's life a little bit worse than it was before.

When you are good, your fairy almost shimmers with pride. She likes to boast about you to other fairies, saying, "My child is so kind and thoughtful. You could not find a prouder fairy than me."

And when you are ready for bed, your fairy sings a little song, especially for you.

Here I am, your fairy friend,
I'll be with you to night's end.
If you're good I'll be so glad,
But I'm sorry when you're bad.

Fairies one and fairies all,
Fairies short and fairies tall,
Fairies gather in a ring,
Hear the song that fairies sing.

If you treat me as you should,
Being kind and being good,
I will love you dearly too,
Always looking after you.

The
Enchanted
Treasure

Many people dream of riches and the power that wealth will bring them. They are sure that all the happiness in the world can be theirs for the price of a gold coin or two. A few have been fortunate enough to find the treasure they seek. Others have been luckier still and have not found it. This is the story of a treasure that passed through many hands before it was lost – perhaps for ever.

A long time ago, a King lived in a castle on a hill. He was interested in only one thing – money. He had a beautiful and loving wife and a little daughter

who was a pretty and clever as any little girl in the kingdom, but he could not feel happy until his coffers were full of gold coins and his treasury was piled high with silver plate.

"Tomorrow," he said to himself, "I will play with my daughter and take a stroll in the garden with my wife, but today I must make sure that the money due in rent from my tenants is properly collected. It is true that I am richer than anyone else I know, but hard times may come, and I must be prepared."

Of course, hard times never came. Tomorrow, which he

would spend with his family, never came either. Day after day, the King worked and schemed to increase his wealth.

One day in early spring, a servant came to the King with a pale and tear-stained face.

"I regret to tell you, Your Highness," he said, "that the Queen, your wife, is gravely ill. She is begging to see you."

The King was stunned. Why, he had seen his wife only yesterday … no, last week … no, a few weeks ago perhaps. All of a sudden, the great love he had for her welled up in his heart, and he rushed to where she lay.

As soon as he saw her lying so still and pale on her bed, the King knew that his wife could not live for long. Clasping her hands in his, he cried out loud, so that his voice could be heard all over the castle.

"Oh, I will give every penny I have," he wailed, "to the person who can give my wife back to me. What is money worth without loved ones to share it with?"

How often we understand what we really care for just as we are about to lose it! Yet the King's offer did not go unanswered. As if from nowhere, a little figure appeared at his elbow. It was a goblin wizard, who had been waiting for just this chance.

"Your Highness," he whispered, "I can save your wife if you will give me the gold you promised."

"Yes, yes," cried the King. "Do what you have to do. Everything I have is yours."

The goblin wizard bent over the bed and spoke softly in the pale woman's ear. "It is as I promised," he said. "All that you wished for is here in this room. Live now and be happy."

The Queen stirred and opened her eyes. Beside the bed, her husband's own eyes filled with tears of happiness. Clasping his wife and daughter to him, he said with great emotion, "I have been a foolish man. We shall be poor for ever now in the things of this world, but we shall be richer in the only things that really matter. I thought that money was all that was of value in the world. Now I realise that time is much more precious – time to enjoy what we have been given, before it is too late."

And so the King and his family pass out of our story, for it is the treasure and its fate that we are following.

The goblin wizard had the golden coins and the silver plate

loaded into chests and placed in seven strong carriages. He knew that he could have taken possession of the castle, too, if he had wished, but he had no interest in anything but real treasure. With a small army of hand-picked soldiers to guard the carriages, he set off for his own country.

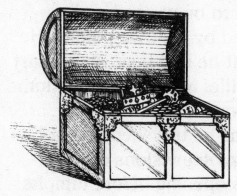

As the carriages rumbled along, the goblin wizard imagined how he would be greeted. Goblins love gold and riches. Surely his countrymen, who had once driven him from their land because of his idle, cunning ways, would welcome him as a long lost brother! More than anything else, the goblin longed to be praised and admired by his own people. He felt that he had been an outcast all his life. Now it was time for his reward.

But as he travelled, the goblin began to see visions of other futures opening before him. As fond as they were of treasure, might his fellow goblins not steal his golden coins from him, laughing at him as they did so? His army, he knew, would flee in the face of the goblin magic they did not understand. He would be alone and defenceless. And what, in those circumstances, would his life be worth? What goblin, dazzled by the treasure in those chests, would hesitate to kill him for such riches?

At that moment, the goblin wizard realised for the first time that he valued his own life much more highly than all the gold he had won.

"It's not worth the risk," he said to himself. "I shall get rid of this treasure as soon as possible. Then I can live safely and without fear. I have not slept for days, knowing that one of my soldiers might try to steal from me. When the treasure has gone, I shall have a night's peace at last."

But losing a very great treasure is not so easy when you want to do it. As many people have found, it is quite easy to lose something you really want to keep, but very difficult to lose the same thing on purpose. First of all, the goblin began giving gold coins to the poor people he

met on the road, but he found
that they began to follow him,
instead of going back to their
homes and improving their lives
as he had hoped. That was no
good at all. In the end, the goblin
had to ask his soldiers to
frighten the people away.

Next, the goblin thought of burying the treasure. Each night, when the soldiers slept, he would take a little spade and bury as many coins as he could beside the road. Some of the little piles of treasure that the goblin buried are still being found to this day.

But the goblin soon realised that it would take years to get rid of all his treasure in this way. He would have to think of something else.

Just as the goblin was becoming ill with worry, and was feeling as though the whole weight of the treasure was on his shoulders, the problem was taken out of his hands.

A gang of robbers was lurking in a nearby wood. When they saw the carriages creaking past, guarded by soldiers, they knew they must contain something very valuable. The next night, under cover of darkness, they attacked!

205

The battle was short and bitter. Before long, all the soldiers lay wounded and beaten by the side of the road. It was a wonder that none of them was killed. The goblin himself had used what little magic he could remember to escape to a nearby mountain top, where he lived to the end of his days, free at last from the burden of wanting what he did not dare to keep.

Meanwhile, the robbers made off with the seven carriages, taking them deep into the forest along tracks that no one else knew. When they reached their camp, many miles away, they forced open the carriages and looked into the chests inside.

Then, for the first time, they realised what a great treasure they had found, and almost immediately, disputes arose between the robbers.

"Five of the seven carriages belong to me!" shouted the robber chief. "I am your leader, and as such I take the greatest share."

"Not so great a share as that!" cried the other robbers. "We shared in the danger. We should share in the treasure, too."

Before long, the arguments grew hot and fierce. Arguments turned to blows. Blows turned to cudgels and swords. By daybreak, not a single robber was left alive in the forest glade.

Year after year, the treasure lay in open chests under the mighty trees. The bodies of the robbers were covered with leaves and gradually sank into the soil, until not even their bones could be seen. But the golden coins remained untarnished, gleaming in the sunlight and the moonlight as night followed day over and over again.

It was a hundred years later that the treasure was found again. The King of the country decided to wage war on his neighbour, who had fairer lands than his own. He knew that the most important battles would be won or lost at sea, so he was determined to build the greatest navy the world had ever seen. He decreed that the great royal forest should be cut down to supply wood for his ships.

Day after day, the woodcutters worked, felling the mighty oaks that had stood for generations. At last they came to the clearing where the treasure lay.

The woodcutters were honest men. They reported their discovery to the King. Needless to say, the King was delighted. As the treasure was found in a royal forest, he declared that it was definitely royal treasure. He ordered his men to load it on to carts and bring it to the great port nearby, where the King had set up his campaign headquarters.

For many months, the worthy woodcutters continued their work. Then the shipwrights took over. Day after day and night after night, the sound of their saws and hammers and chisels could be heard for miles around.

At last the great fleet sat proudly in the water, its pennants flying. The navy was ready to sail.

As the King prepared to go on board, he realised that he had a problem. He dared not leave his great treasure behind, for he feared that it would be stolen in his absence. After all, he would be taking his army with him. There would be no one left behind to guard the treasure.

"There is only one thing to be done," said the King. "I shall have to take the treasure with me." He ordered his men to load it all on to the greatest ship in the fleet. Then he went on board himself and gave the order to set sail. With a fair wind, the fleet left the harbour.

At first all went well as the mighty galleons sailed across the calm sea, but then a great wind blew up, whipping the waves into peaks higher than the tallest mast. Most of the fleet was blown back to the harbour, where the sailors and soldiers scrambled ashore. But the flagship of the fleet lay heavy in the water with the weight of the treasure on board. She soon began to sink lower and lower, as seawater flooded her decks and holds. The waves towered above her.

The King, clinging to the mast, cried out as another had done before him. "I will give all my treasure, if only I can be saved from this terrible fate! Why, oh why, did I decide to wage war when I could have stayed safely at home?" This time, no passing goblin arrived to save the day. The ship went down, and the King went with it. The caskets of treasure spilled out on to the sandy sea bed.

And that is where they lie now, their contents glittering in the green water. Would it have made a difference to any of the people who came into contact with the treasure if they had known that it was enchanted? Long, long ago, a curse had been put upon the gold and silver.

> *You shall not*
> > *Give lasting pleasure,*
> *But teach what is*
> > *A life's true measure.*

Which of those who saw the glitter of the gold could have walked away from its glow? Would you?

The Lost
Book

I don't suppose there is anyone who has not, at some time or another, lost something they value. It is always distressing, whether it is a single sock or a diamond ring. Sometimes the loss is of something that simply cannot be replaced. That is what happened to Wizard Midnight.

Now Wizard Midnight was not a careless man. He could hardly have been a wizard if he were, for using spells is very detailed work. One slip in the recipe of a spell – a hair from the back of a polar bear instead of a grizzly bear, for example – and disaster can be the result. Many an apprentice wizard has simply disappeared because he did not pay careful attention to the instructions in his *Great Book of Wizardry*.

No, Wizard Midnight was always careful, and he took his work very seriously. He was not one of these up-and-coming wizards who are more interested in clouds of yellow and red smoke than in real magic. But Midnight had been a wizard for a very long time, and that meant that his spellatory (like a laboratory, but for spells) was packed from floor to ceiling with boxes and caskets and jars and – most of all – books.

The names of the books would give you some idea of the many areas of magic that Wizard Midnight had studied. *Princes into Frogs: an illustrated guide* rubbed shoulders with *Verses and Curses: favourite rhymes from the Great Wizards*. At the bottom of a dusty pile near the door, you might find *A Spell Too Far: an unauthorised biography of Wizard Twilight (disappeared)*. Propping up the broken leg of the wizard's chair you might see *Invisibility: a guide for larger wizards*.

Yes, Wizard Midnight was certainly a very well-read wizard, but what he really needed was a secretary or a librarian to help him keep his books in order. There had been a young elf who had helped him once, but really he had been more trouble than he was worth. Several spells had gone seriously wrong because of mistakes he had made. After that, Wizard Midnight decided to work alone.

It was late one night when the wizard made his first Really Big Mistake. The spellatory was lit only by a flickering candle. Wizard Midnight was tired, but he did just want to finish the spell he was working on before he went to bed. He knew that if he did not, he would toss and turn all night with the spell on his mind.

The spell he was working on was quite a small one, but it would be very, very useful to mothers everywhere, so the wizard was keen to complete it as soon as possible. It was a spell for making babies love all the foods that are really good for them, such as vegetables. At last the wizard felt that the spell was right. It would have to be tested, of course, before it could be used on real babies, but he was pretty sure that there would be no unpleasant side effects.

Before he went to bed, the wizard wrote the new spell in the most important book in his library. It was his own special spell book, so important that it didn't even have a name on the cover. It was the book that contained all the spells the wizard found essential every day. Wizard Midnight wrote down the new spell. He signed it with his name and the date, as all wizards are encouraged to do when they first begin to make spells. Then he put down the book and went to bed.

How easy it is to write that! "He put down the book" we say, and it sounds so simple. It *was* so simple. What was not simple was finding the book again next morning, as you will see.

Wizard Midnight rose next morning bright and early. As usual, he decided to begin the day with a little light breakfast of acorn cereal and daisy juice. He didn't go out and pick what he needed for his breakfast. Of course not! He was a wizard! All that was needed was a quick spell over his bowl and cup. But the spell was in the special spell book, and the special spell book was... It began to seem as if things would not be easy.

Yes, where was that book? The wizard remembered as clearly as anything putting it down the night before. It must be somewhere near his chair. But which of the chairs in the spellatory had he been sitting on last night? It was really rather difficult to remember.

Never mind. The wizard knew a simple little spell for finding

any book in his library. He had
spent three or four weeks
inventing it after the impossible
elf had been sent on his way. At
least, when I say that the wizard
"knew" the spell, I mean that he
had it written down, so that he
could use it at a moment's
notice. And where was it written?
Oh dear…

"I am a wizard," said Midnight
to himself. "I can and I will find a
way out of this mess. But first I
really must have some
breakfast."

There was nothing for it.
Midnight had to go outside and
gather some toadstools with his

own hands. His special spell for
making sure they were not
poisonous was in his special
spell book, so he had to think
carefully about it and then just
hope for the best. (Don't try this
yourselves unless you know the
antidote spell, as Wizard
Midnight did.)

Getting breakfast without
magic took much more time than
usual. Wizard Midnight found
that half the morning had
disappeared before he was able
to start looking for his spell
book. Now where was that book?

All day the wizard searched.
He stared at the titles of his

books until they began to dance in front of his eyes. Surely he had just seen *Wizardry for Beginners* in another pile? He must be getting confused. (In fact, the wizard was not getting confused at all. He had two copies of *Wizardry for Beginners* because both his grandmothers had given him the book when he first went to wizard school.)

That night, Wizard Midnight went to bed with a heavy heart. Where could that book be?

It was beginning to cross his mind for the first time that something more than simple carelessness might have happened to the book.

What, for example, if another wizard had crept in while Wizard Midnight slept and spirited the book away? What if a magic spell, cast hundreds of miles away, had misfired and made his book invisible? What if a jealous witch, eager to get her own back for being beaten in last year's Master Magician Contest, had sent her black cat to "borrow" the book? The more Wizard Midnight thought about it, the more sure he was that there had been some malicious magic done.

What could he do about it? It is almost impossible to reverse a spell if you do not know what the first spell was. It is definitely impossible if you do not even know for sure that a spell has been used in the first place.

Wizard Midnight thought and thought. He couldn't sleep and he couldn't eat. Only one thing ran through his mind. At all costs, he must get that book back. Not only was his life's work between those covers, but he dreaded to think what would happen if the book fell into the wrong hands.

It took Wizard Midnight two weeks of concentrated thinking and worrying to come up with an idea. He couldn't undo whatever spell had been put on him or his book, but he could go back in time to the last moment he had held the book in his hands. It would be a difficult spell – time travelling is one of the hardest branches of magic – but not impossible. Wizard Midnight decided to start work right away.

The spell took much longer to develop than was usually the case. The wizard's special spell book had contained many useful hints and tips, as well as a number of important short cuts. This time, Wizard Midnight had to manage without any of them.

It was spring when Wizard Midnight lost his book, but it was autumn when he finally finished his time-reversing spell. Brown leaves were beginning to rustle under his door as he prepared to try his spell.

Obviously, I cannot tell you the whole spell, but some of it went like this:

The pages of the book of time
Turn as each night follows day,
Turn them back again in rhyme
And past and present fade away.

Trembling with excitement, the wizard recited the whole spell. There was a shimmering strangeness in the spellatory, and he suddenly found himself sitting late at night, his special spell book in his hands and a daffodil in a vase on his desk.

What did the wizard do next? He looked down at his newly written baby-food spell. He was very tired. He put down his book...

What more can I tell you of Wizard Midnight? In his spellatory, spring becomes summer, and summer becomes autumn. And autumn becomes spring. Winter – and the future – never come.

The
Flying
Carpet

What do you give a wizard who has everything for his birthday? Any wizard worth his salt can magic whatever he needs at any time of day or night. It is pointless giving him socks or boxes of chocolates or aftershave. (Most wizards grow beards in any case, so there isn't any *shave* to come *after*.)

The only thing you can really give a wizard is something new in the magic line – a book of spells, perhaps, or a special magic stirring stick. That is why a little elf called Esmerelda went into Mrs Magglepaggle's Magic Shop one Saturday morning.

"I'm looking for a birthday present for my uncle," she explained. "He's a wizard, and it's so hard to find him anything he couldn't magic up for himself."

"My dear, I know just what you mean," replied Mrs Magglepaggle, who was such a good saleswoman she could have sold ears to elves. "I have just the same trouble," she went on, "with my old grandfather. Have you considered something in the clothing line? Many wizards are wearing old-fashioned robes that do nothing for their figures. What about a new elasticated wizard suit?"

She showed Esmerelda a rather garish creation in shiny green stretchy stuff, with a pattern of stars around the hem.

"I don't quite see Uncle Albertus in that," said the little elf. "I was thinking more of something to help him with his magic."

"Seven-league boots?" suggested Mrs Magglepaggle. "They're coming back into fashion in a big

way, even if we don't have leagues
any more. Or what about a nice
new wand? These ones are made
of aluminium – so much lighter
to carry."

"No, no," cried Esmerelda. She
was beginning to think that it
had been a mistake to come into
the shop. She looked around at
the shelves and noticed what
looked like a rolled-up rug in a
corner at the back.

"What is that, please?" she
asked politely.

Mrs Magglepaggle rolled out
the carpet with one swift
movement. It looked as though a
mouse had been nibbling one

corner, and the colours were rather faded.

"As you can see," said the saleswoman, "it has seen better days, which is why I could let you have it at a very reasonable price. Normally, a carpet like this would cost you a king's ransom. At one time, it was a magic carpet, capable of flying all over the world, but it has lost almost all its magic. The best it can manage now is a little hover around the level of your knees. It gets exhausted after five minutes and flops down again."

"I see," said Esmerelda slowly. In truth, she felt rather sorry for the carpet, and she liked the pattern. "I'll take it," she said firmly, "but I shall want a large discount for wear and tear."

Mrs Magglepaggle did drop the price a good deal. She felt that the carpet made her shop look rather shabby, and although she had sold quite a lot of secondhand magic items at one time, she had decided recently to concentrate on new things. There was more demand for them.

Esmerelda took the carpet home and wrapped it up in lots and lots of silver paper. Then she carried it carefully to her uncle's woodland house.

"Happy Birthday, Uncle Albertus!" she called, as she pushed open the front door.

Uncle Albertus was relaxing in his favourite chair. He was not a very energetic wizard. He felt that he deserved a rest on his birthday. However, he jumped to his feet when he saw his little niece and the bulky parcel she was carrying.

"My dear, you shouldn't have!" he cried, running to help her. "I hope you haven't spent too much of your pocket money on your old uncle."

"No, I haven't," said Esmerelda, perhaps with more truth than politeness. "It didn't cost very much because it's old."

Uncle Albertus was busy undoing the paper. As he rolled out the carpet he gave a little gasp. "My dear, do you know what we have here? It's a genuine, first class, original Arabian flying carpet."

"Is that good?" asked Esmerelda, who knew very little about carpets. "I'm afraid it's not much use, as it doesn't fly very much any more."

"Of course it doesn't," replied her uncle, his eyes gleaming. "No carpet can fly in this condition. It needs a good cleaning and a little magic thread to mend these holes. Then, my dear, it will be as good as new and a very special carpet indeed. Come back tomorrow, when I have had a chance to do a little work on it. Then you will see something extraordinary."

Esmerelda did not need much encouragement. She was so very

pleased to have given her uncle something he really liked. And she was eager to see the new carpet in action.

Next morning, she arrived early at her uncle's house. She found him with a duster around his head and a carpet beater in his hand. He made a rather grand gesture with the carpet beater in the direction of his ceiling. Esmerelda looked up. There was the carpet, as large as life. It was floating just below the ceiling, its colours gleaming and its little mouse holes now invisible. As she watched, the little elf saw the magic carpet shake itself vigorously, like a puppy coming out of a pond.

"Yes, it's very frisky this morning," said Uncle Albertus. "Would you like to try it? I'll just call it down. Now where's my Arabic phrase book?"

Esmerelda didn't understand what he said next, but it sounded quite impressive. "It's what you use to hail a taxi in Cairo," explained her uncle, "but it seems to work with carpets too. Hop on!"

Esmerelda quite expected the carpet to flop to the floor under the weight of an elf and a rather large uncle, but it felt quite firm and energetic as she sat down, rather like a powerful horse.

"Are you ready?" asked Uncle Albertus. "Hold on tight. It may be quite vigorous to begin with."

With a flip and a flap, the carpet zoomed out of the door and high up into the air.

"Where are we going?" shouted Esmerelda, above the noise of the wind.

"Wherever we like!" called her uncle. "All we have to do is to think of where we want to be!"

Esmerelda at once thought of a rather beautiful beach she had once visited on holiday. At once the carpet began to spin. Round and round it went, until the little elf was dizzy and wishing she could get off.

"Stop thinking!" called her uncle. "We're both thinking of different places and the carpet doesn't know which way to go."

Esmerelda was so dizzy now that she could hardly think anyway. At once, the carpet stopped spinning and set off at a steady pace in a northerly direction instead.

"I've always wanted to visit the North Pole!" called her uncle, "but you need terribly strong magic in cold places. I was never quite able to manage it before."

"But it will be cold!" objected Esmerelda, whose beach had been wonderfully warm and sunny.

"Don't worry," cried her uncle, doing a quick bit of magic. At once, they were both dressed in warm clothes and holding hot water bottles to be on the safe side. "That's the sort of magic I can manage," laughed Uncle Albertus.

The North Pole, when they reached it, was a little bit of a disappointment. There was nothing there but ice and snow in every direction.

"I thought there would be polar bears," said Esmerelda,

"and a sort of signpost, pointing south, you know."

"So did I," said Uncle Albertus. "Ah well, time to go home, my dear, I suppose."

This time, with both of them thinking of the same place, the carpet travelled at double-quick speed. In no time at all, they were back in Uncle Albertus' house.

"Time for a cup of dandelion tea!" cried the wizard, waving his wand. "Will you be mother?"

Esmerelda laughed and picked up the teapot. It was rather unfortunate that just at that moment the carpet decided to give a shimmy and a shake. The poor little elf dropped the teapot and hot tea splashed all over the magic carpet.

If carpets can be said to yelp, that's exactly what this carpet did. In less time that it takes to read this sentence, it had whisked itself out from under their feet and hurtled out of the door. Uncle Albertus fished out his Arabic phrase book and tried saying "a thousand, thousand pardons" and "forgive your unworthy servant", but the carpet did not return.

"I'm afraid we've seen the last of it," said the wizard with a sigh. "It was bound to happen. Those thoroughbred carpets are very highly strung. But it was a wonderful present, my dear, and I thoroughly enjoyed my trip to the North Pole, even if there weren't any polar bears."

Apparently, the carpet has been sighted in several parts of the world since that day. If you should happen to hop on it by mistake one day, hold on tight and think hard of where you would like to go. Oh … and do try not to drop tea on it!

The
Friendly
Dragon

Everyone knows that most dragons are not friendly. They breathe fire for one thing, which is never comfortable for those near them. After all, even if he isn't trying to burn you to a frazzle, a dragon might become absentminded just for a moment and forget not to breathe. It would only take a sort of a snort to turn you into toast.

Because dragons are known to be a problem for ordinary mortals, most people keep well clear of them. It's not hard to find out where they are living, for their caves always look rather burnt around the edges and smell of smoke. People in nearby towns and villages know which hillsides to avoid and always consult their noses about the smokiness of the air before they go along a forest path.

This was all very well in the days when there was a dragon on every mountain. From time to time, dragons would get together and exchange ideas. Then smoke would rise from the mountains as their hot breaths mingled in the air above.

But in recent years, there have been fewer and fewer dragons. Some say that they are related to the ancient dinosaurs, who once roamed our earth. Like them, they will all die out in time.

Others say that all dragons have learned to live underground, where they sometimes make the earth shake. Whatever is happening, there simply are not so many dragons about these days, which is a relief in lots of ways.

It is very rare now for a laundry woman to find that all her washing has been scorched on the line. On the other hand, there are more forest fires than there used to be. Dragons were very good at sniffing a different kind of smoke on the air, and would go and stamp out any smouldering timbers with their big feet. Nowadays, that hardly ever happens, and the fire is fanned until huge trees catch alight.

All of this means that life is much harder for the few remaining dragons than it used to be. People in nearby villages have forgotten how to live with a dragon in their neighbourhood, and dragons have become rather lonely. The chances of getting together with other dragons are very slim now. A dragon might spend hundreds of years on his own, spending his days and nights alone without ever seeing a fire-breathing brother.

That is exactly what happened
not so long ago near the village
of Frazzle in the Wild Mountains.
Those mountains were not so
very wild at the time of this
story, but they did still have one
single dragon living in a cave
near the top. Everyone knew he
was there, but as they saw no
sign of him for year after year,
there were always rumours flying
about that he had died at last.

Then, of course, a few brave
lads would climb up the
mountain to check, for everyone
knows that each dragon keeps a
hoard of gold deep in his cave.
To get hold of the gold, you have

to wait until the dragon has died, or be prepared to fight him for it. Dragon-fighting is not taught in our military schools today, so it is a long time since a knight tackled a real dragon.

As they climbed, the lads would look out for signs of dragon activity – twigs that were broken or scorched, for example. Always they came back to the village, saying, "We didn't see him, but he's definitely still there."

As time passed, the dragon grew more and more lonely. He used to spend hour after hour happily counting his gold and warming its cold surfaces with the fire from his nostrils. Now, even that activity was beginning to bore him. It seemed so empty somehow.

What this dragon really wanted was a friend – someone he could discuss fire-breathing and compare gold pieces with. But he knew perfectly well that there was not another dragon for miles around. There was only one thing for it. He would have to find a human friend.

The dragon was pretty sure that humans were interested in fire and gold too. He thought he might be able to find someone who would like to come for a chat now and then. In return, he might be able to do something useful for them. He could heat-strip their paintwork perhaps, when they wanted to redecorate, or heat their bath water when there was a power cut.

With this in mind, the dragon set off bright and early one morning for the nearby village.

It was not encouraging that the very first person he came across flew screaming into his house at the first sight of the dragon's green and yellow face.

"Never mind," said the dragon to himself. "There will be some braver people in the village. Not everyone likes dragons. I do understand that. Not all dragons like humans, after all."

But as the dragon approached the village, more and more people ran screaming from him. It was unheard of for a dragon to come into a town or village. They were sure that they were all about to be burnt in their beds.

The dragon hung around in the main square for a while. He even tried peering in a few windows. No one came out at all. After a while, he trotted unhappily back towards the mountain.

As soon as he had gone, there was great activity in the village. A meeting was called in the main square, and everyone got together to decide what must be done.

Desperately, they turned first to old Angus.

"You're the only person still alive who received the old dragon-fighting training," they said. "You must go and fight him, so that he doesn't come back."

"Don't be ridiculous," cried Angus. "I'm eighty-five! I can't go fighting dragons at my age! Besides, he looked like quite a young dragon to me – two or three hundred years old at the most – he could run rings round me any day."

There was some sense in Angus' words, but no one could think of anything else to do. At least, not anything sensible.

"We could build a great big wooden fence around the village," said one bright spark, "so that he couldn't get in."

"And where would be get the wood from?" asked Angus.

"Why, the forest, of course."

"And where is the forest?"

"Don't be silly. It's all over the mountain."

"And who lives at the top of the mountain?"

"Oh…"

Other suggestions were no better. Could they somehow put out the dragon's fire with water from a hose? Could they sneak up one night and put bars across his cave? Could they send someone out to dig a big pit that he could fall into? All these ideas met with the same problem. No one was brave enough to volunteer to go and carry them out.

At last a little voice piped up. It was a little boy who was new to the village. He had come to live with his aunt the year before and knew what it was like to feel an outsider and alone.

"I think," he said, "that I could just talk to the dragon. You know, have a chat and find out why he came down from his cave. Then we'll know what to do."

That sounded a sillier idea than all the others put together, but it was the only idea that had a volunteer attached to it. Before long, the villagers had agreed. Next morning, the little boy would climb up to the dragon's cave at the top of the mountain and have a few words with him.

"We'll never see him again," said Angus, shaking his head. "But if the boy wants to go…" Deep down, everyone wondered if the dragon had been just a tiny bit hungry. They used to eat princesses, didn't they, in the old days? They were pretty sure that the boy was about to become breakfast.

But next morning, the boy found that he would not need to climb the mountain. For the dragon once again came wandering through the village. When he sat down in the middle of the main square, the boy went bravely out to meet him.

"Hello," said the boy, politely.

"Hello," said the dragon. "Er … I'm a dragon."

"I know," said the boy. "I'm called Tom."

"Oh, I'm Sxbvfnxzs," said the friendly dragon.

"I don't think I can pronounce that," said Tom. "May I just call you Dragon?"

"Certainly," said Sxbvfnxzs.

"The thing is," said Tom, "we were wondering why you came to visit us yesterday. And today."

"It's a little hard to explain…" began the dragon, but he did.

For several hours, the dragon and the boy sat in the square and talked. "What's happening out there?" asked the villagers behind their curtains. "Has he eaten him yet?"

But Tom and the dragon were having a perfectly friendly conversation. Towards the end of the afternoon, the dragon gave Tom a jolly smile and ambled off back to his cave.

At once, all the villagers rushed out and surrounded the boy.

"What did he say?"

"What took you so long?"

"Does he speak English?"

"Will he be back?"

Tom held up his hand. "He speaks English," he said, "and, yes, he will be back. He's rather lonely up on his mountain, now that there are no other dragons to visit. He'd like to come down to the village sometimes for a chat. Once a year would be fine, he says, as time goes much more quickly for dragons than it does for us."

The villagers were stunned. A friendly dragon on their doorsteps? Who had ever heard of such a thing? The Mayor's eyes began to gleam. This might be the biggest tourist attraction of all time. Visit Frazzle and Dine with Dragons!

"But he would like his visits to be absolutely secret," Tom went on firmly.

The Mayor's face fell. "Isn't there any room for … er … negotiation here?" he asked.

"Well," said Tom, "he could burn down a few of our houses instead if you like."

"No, no, no," said the Mayor. "Absolute secrecy will be fine."

And that is how the matter was left. The dragon was happy. Tom was happy. Even the Mayor was happy. What's that? No, I'm afraid you won't find Frazzle on any map. Absolute secrecy is absolute secrecy after all!

The Conjuror's Secret

Mr Wizzy packed his bags carefully. He always made a last-minute check of all his equipment before he went to a performance. It would be a disaster if he cried "Hey presto!" and there were no flowers *up* his sleeve to come bursting *out*! For Mr Wizzy was a conjuror.

Now there are conjurors and conjurors. Some do wonderful tricks and hold you spellbound as they make things appear and disappear. Long strings of coloured flags are pulled out of their mouths. Clouds of blue smoke appear as they finish a trick. Sometimes they even seem to be able to tell what you are thinking, as they guess what is in your pockets or which card you have chosen.

But you know, those tricks are just that – tricks. They are the result of years and years of practice, but if you had the time and wanted to badly enough, you could learn to do most of those tricks yourself.

Some conjurors are different. They do *real* magic. Yes, they really do make things appear and disappear. The things don't just *seem* to be there or not there. They have really appeared out of nothing or actually disappeared into thin air. And if those magicians seem to know what you are thinking, look out!

As you probably know, there are lots and lots of the first kind of conjuror. You may well have been to a party or a show where one has performed. But the *real* magicians are very few and far between. Sometimes you may not even realise that you have met one.

Mr Wizzy was the second kind of conjuror. He had special powers, which he took very seriously. Early on in his career, when he first realised that he really could do magic, Mr Wizzy made a solemn vow. He promised to use his magic only to give people pleasure, never to get things for himself or to harm anyone. And up to the point where this story begins, he had always kept his promise. It was when he broke it – just once – that things began to go wrong.

We left Mr Wizzy carefully packing things for his show that afternoon. He was due to appear in the children's ward of the local hospital. It was almost Christmas, and Mr Wizzy had been booked to give the children a special treat. Most of them would not be able to go home for

Christmas, so the nurses and doctors always tried to make things extra special on the ward.

As Mr Wizzy was getting ready, his doorbell rang.

"Well, dash my buttons," said Mr Wizzy, "who can that be, just as I'm getting ready?"

He hurried to the front door, trying to tie his bow tie with one hand as he went.

Standing on the doorstep was Mr Wizzy's next-door neighbour, Mrs Bizzybee. She was the most talkative woman for miles around, and Mr Wizzy gave a little groan as he saw her standing there.

"Oh, Mr Wizzy," said Mrs Bizzybee, "I-do-hope-you-don't-mind-me-disturbing-you-in-the-middle-of-the-afternoon-like-this-but-my-cat-Whiskers-you-know-the-one-with-a-black-face-and-a-brown-body-and-a-white-tip-to-his-tail-not-the-one-with-the-little-pink-face-and-white-socks-that's-Angelica-not-Whiskers-oh-but-Whiskers-has-gone-missing-and-I-can't-find-him-anywhere-and-I'm-so-very-afraid-he-may-have-gone-on-to-that-busy-main-road-not-the-one-going-to-Elmville-but-the-other-one-you-know-the-one-going-to-Turnytown-and-I-don't-know-what-to-do-can-you-help?"

Phew! That's just how Mrs Bizzybee talked, without taking a breath. By the time she had finished, Mr Wizzy felt exhausted and he hadn't the faintest idea what she wanted him to do.

Mrs Bizzybee took a deep breath. Mr Wizzy could see that she was just about to begin all over again. She must be stopped at all costs! Mr Wizzy began talking just as fast as she had, just to keep her quiet.

"Oh, Mrs Bizzybee," he said, rushing through to his sitting room and picking up his conjuring case and the basket with his animal helpers, "I'm-not-sure-what-you-want-me-to-do-to-help-but-I-haven't-got-time-to-stop-so-I'll-just-er-think-very-hard-about-it-like-this-*Wizzy-Kizzy-help-Mrs-Bizzy-give-her-everything-she-wants!*-and-now-I-must-go-perhaps-you-can-shut-the-front-door-for-me-oh-thank-you-goodbye!"

Double phew! In his hurry to get out of the house and away from Mrs Bizzybee, Mr Wizzy had forgotten his own most important rule. He had said a little spell to make everything all right for his neighbour, but he hadn't really done it to help her. He had done it for his own convenience so that he could get away quickly.

As Mr Wizzy drove away, he didn't even think about what he had done. In fact, he had said the spell so quickly that he hadn't concentrated properly on the words. He hadn't simply asked for Mrs Bizzybee to find her missing cat, he had asked for her to have *everything* she wanted!

It is a pity that Mr Wizzy didn't look in his mirror as he sped down the road. He would have seen Mrs Bizzybee standing on his doorstep in absolute amazement, with Whiskers in her arms, several diamond tiaras on

her head and weighing about half
as much as she had two minutes
before. Things became even
more confusing for Mrs Bizzybee
when she got home five minutes
later to find that each of her
three daughters suddenly found
herself the proud mother of
twins, so that Mrs Bizzybee had
all the grandchildren she had
ever longed for.

Now you can see as well as I
can that this kind of magic is
disastrous. What kind of a world
would it be if anyone who could
do magic just said the first thing
that came into his or her head,
as Mr Wizzy had just done?

Mr Wizzy, however, was as yet unaware of the havoc he had left behind him. He arrived at the hospital in good time and carried his conjuring case and basket into the children's ward.

The nurses had kindly pulled the curtains across at the end of the ward, so that Mr Wizzy could get all his things ready without the children seeing. Once again, the conjuror checked his equipment. In the back of his mind, he had just the tiniest feeling that something was a little bit wrong, but he couldn't for the life of him think what it was. To tell you the truth, in spite of his many years of experience, Mr Wizzy always got rather nervous before a performance. That is perhaps why he was not thinking straight as he prepared to give his show.

At last it was time for the magic show to begin. Mr Wizzy made a noise like a trumpet fanfare, and the nurses whisked back the curtains. How the children clapped and cheered when they saw Mr Wizzy. They did not know that things were about to go badly wrong.

Mr Wizzy always liked to start his act with a bang – a real bang. As usual, he threw his top hat up into the air, clapped his hands and … the hat dropped to the ground and rolled away under the nearest bed.

Well, of course, that is not at all what was supposed to happen. When Mr Wizzy clapped his hands, he always said a little disappearing spell, and the hat just vanished into thin air. Mr Wizzy was pretty sure that he had got the spell right. He couldn't understand why it didn't work.

The show must go on, and Mr Wizzy was nothing if not professional. With a flourish, he reached into his coat and pulled out … his handkerchief. Oh dear, that was wrong too. It shouldn't have been a handkerchief that appeared but a white dove, which would flutter up to the ceiling and sit quietly nearby until it was time to go home with the conjuror.

Mr Wizzy was becoming quite flustered now. Over the years, he had begun to use more and more real magic in his act, so that he relied on it a good deal. His ordinary conjuring skills were really quite rusty. Mr Wizzy felt a sinking feeling in his tummy. He was pretty sure now that he knew what was happening, and it was something quite, quite dreadful. Mr Wizzy had completely lost his magic powers!

Mr Wizzy looked very red as he glanced at the children's expectant faces. He couldn't for the life of him think what to do. The full horror of the situation was just breaking upon him, and for the first time, he knew *exactly* why it was happening.

If only he hadn't used that silly spell on Mrs Bizzybee. He had broken his promise, and as a result, his magic had deserted him. Mr Wizzy thought with dread of the situation he might find when he got home. He now realised how hasty he had been in casting Mrs Bizzybee's spell. He couldn't remember exactly what he had said, but he was pretty sure that the results could spell the end of his life as a conjuror for ever.

Mr Wizzy gazed miserably at his audience. They looked back at him, waiting for a wonderful trick. Then, suddenly, they all began to laugh and clap their hands. Mr Wizzy was confused for a moment, then he looked down and saw with amazement that his white rabbit, Alonso, was doing a tap dance on the table top!

Mr Wizzy was a natural showman, but he was so stunned by the sight of his tap-dancing rabbit that he didn't know what to do. Then the rabbit hissed at him out of the corner of his mouth, "Music! Give me some music!" Almost mechanically, Mr Wizzy began to sing in time with the rabbit's dancing. The children could hardly believe their eyes as the rabbit did a triple somersault with twist as the climax of his dance. Then he bowed several times to his audience, and Mr Wizzy, coming to his senses at last, smiled and bowed too.

"And now," said Mr Wizzy grandly, " Alonso the Magnificent will perform another amazing trick! Take it away, Alonso!"

Alonso extended his right paw. Mr Wizzy hesitated for a moment, then placed his magic wand in the rabbit's grasp. Alonso waved the wand once, twice, three times, and a shower of little stars fell from the ceiling on to the heads of the children watching. It was lovely to see them laugh and stretch up their little hands to try to catch the falling sparklers. But the stars were like bubbles. As soon as they touched something, they vanished.

The rabbit bowed again. Then he waved his wand and pointed to Mr Wizzy's pocket. This time, Mr Wizzy picked up his cue straight away. He felt in his pocket and pulled out a red flag, and a yellow flag, and a blue flag, and a white flag, and a green flag … on and on and on, until there were flags stretching from one end of the ward to the other.

"Ladies and gentlemen, boys and girls, it is time for the grand finale," cried Mr Wizzy, wondering what the rabbit could possibly find to do for this. Usually, Mr Wizzy took the opportunity to say a quick spell and make himself vanish in a puff of green smoke. Then there would be a drum roll, and he would reappear at the other end of the room.

As Mr Wizzy finished his announcement, the rabbit waved his paw and the whole ward disappeared. Mr Wizzy, the children, the doctors, the nurses and the rabbit found themselves sitting on a grassy bank outside in the warm sunshine. This was all the more extraordinary as it had been a grey, cold day outside only five minutes before.

The illusion lasted only for a minute. Then everyone was back in the ward and the audience was clapping and cheering more loudly than any audience had ever applauded Mr Wizzy before.

"More! More! More!" cried the children, stamping their feet. Their cheeks were pink and their eyes were bright. All of them looked much, much better than they had when Mr Wizzy arrived.

But Mr Wizzy knew better than to push his luck. He packed up his things and waved to the children. Then he hurried home in his little car.

Mr Wizzy dreaded to think what he would see as he approached his house. Sure enough, Mrs Bizzybee's home was surrounded by vans with aerials on top and dozens of eager reporters were hammering at the door. Clearly, the extraordinary things that had happened to Mrs Bizzybee were secret no more. Soon *everyone* would know.

Mr Wizzy crept into his house through the back door. He had no wish to see his face all over that evening's television news programmes. As usual, he put away his equipment and opened the basket with his animal helpers, so that they could hop and fly about freely in the conjuror's sitting room.

"Only," said Mr Wizzy sadly to himself, "I'm not a conjuror any more. If only I hadn't said that stupid spell. Now I don't even have my magic to try to put things right. Whatever am I going to do?"

"I could do it," said the rabbit.

Mr Wizzy rubbed his eyes. He was so miserable that the events at the hospital had become a great blur in his mind. Now he remembered the amazing tricks that the rabbit had done. (And in case you're wondering, the rabbit never had spoken until that day.)

"I could probably put things right," said the rabbit again.

Mr Wizzy made a big effort to concentrate. "I don't understand," he said. "What has happened?"

"Most people don't realise," said the rabbit, "that there is always the same amount of magic in the world. It may pass from one person to another, but it does not grow greater or less. When your magic left you because of the spell on Mrs Bizzybee, I was the nearest creature who could use it properly, so it came to me. After all, I've been watching you do your tricks for *years*. What do you think of my show so far?"

"It was wonderful," said Mr Wizzy. "I particularly liked the falling stars. They were truly magical, I thought. One or two parts could do with a little more polish, perhaps, but we could work on those together. Oh!"

"Yes?" said the rabbit.

"Well, I just realised how things are going to be from now on. I'll be *your* assistant, instead of the other way round."

"That's right," said the rabbit, "and in time, maybe some of the magic will start slipping back from me to you. Who knows?"

Mr Wizzy slumped back in his chair with relief. It was going to be all right. He would still be able to cheer people up and make them smile, he just wouldn't be playing the same part.

"No time to relax now!" cried the rabbit. "We still have to sort out the muddle with Mrs Bizzybee. We can't leave things as they are."

"No, of course not," replied the ex-conjuror. "I have thought about it, but the only idea I had was to wind back time so that none of what happened this afternoon really happened."

"No," said the rabbit, "that won't be possible. That would mean that you never said the silly spell, so you never lost your magic powers. I'm not allowed to do that. But I did have another idea. We could simply do a forgetting spell so that no one remembers that anything strange happened. And maybe a bit of a remembering-wrong spell so that the awkward bits are tidied up."

"But won't that take away *your* magic," asked Mr Wizzy.

"No," said the rabbit. "Mrs Bizzybee is terribly worried at the moment that *she* can't remember what happened. This will sort it all out for her."

So the rabbit said a spell rather quietly, so that Mr Wizzy couldn't hear, and from the window they watched as the television and news reporters drove away, scratching their heads.

The next moment, Mrs Bizzybee rang the front door bell – several times!

Mr Wizzy found himself shaking in his shoes as he went to answer it. As usual, his neighbour began talking as soon as he opened the door.

"Oh-Mr-Wizzy-I-haven't-had-a-minute-to-myself-since-that-incredible-lottery-win-I-felt-I-just-had-to-step-across-and-say-hello-what-do-you-think-of-me-now-that-month-on-a-health-farm-did-me-the-world-of-good-and-I-did-buy-one-or-two-little-bits-and-pieces-for-myself-but-of-course-most-of-the-money-will-be-going-to-the-twins-such-a-surprise-but-everyone-is-delighted-all-my-girls-wanted-children-as-much-as-I-wanted-grandchildren-but-*three*-sets-of-twins-well-it's-amazing-only-they-do-run-in-my-family-you-know-oh-yes-my-Great-Uncle-Barneybee-was-a-twin-and-so-now-I-come-to-think-of-it-was…"

"Mrs Bizzybee, I'm *delighted*," said Mr Wizzy quickly, as Mrs Bizzybee drew breath. "Now I know what a busy grandmother you must be, so I'll come round tomorrow to hear *all* about it."

Exhausted, Mr Wizzy staggered back to the sitting room, where the rabbit was having a nice chat with the dove about the best place to hide during the tricks.

"Everything is all right," said the ex-conjuror. "I don't quite understand what she was talking about when she mentioned twins, but never mind. Now what I need is a nice cup of tea."

Mr Wizzy was just about to get up and go into the kitchen, when he found that he already had a steaming cup of tea in his hand!

The rabbit gave him a wink. "It was to give *you* pleasure," he said, "so I was able to do it."

"You know," smiled Mr Wizzy, "I believe I like this arrangement better than the last one!"

The Christmas Pudding Wish

Once upon a time there was a little boy who wanted more than anything else to have a baby brother. He would mention it casually to his parents as often as he dared.

"What a pity," he would say, as he looked at the seesaw in the park, "that I don't have a little brother to play on *that* with. It would be so much fun."

Or when his parents were taking him shopping, he would look at toys in the shop windows and say, wistfully, "That drum is much too young for *me*, but it would be perfect for a much smaller boy, wouldn't it?"

But although his parents smiled and even sometimes laughed at his comments, he never seemed to be any nearer to having a little baby brother.

Freddie, for that was his name, remembered that Georgia at playgroup had told him about her own little brother being born. "I didn't know what was happening," she said, "but there was a lot of whispering one night and Mum didn't want any supper. Then, in the morning, there he was, tucked up in a cot beside Mum's bed."

After that, Freddie kept a sharp eye on his mother. "Are you sure you feel hungry?" he would ask her. "Wouldn't you rather go without supper tonight? You're not exactly *thin,* you know."

"Yes, I definitely do want supper!" laughed his mother, "and no more comments about how fat I am, if you don't mind! I must have a little word with you about that in any case."

But Freddie had rushed off to play with his toys. He really wasn't very interested while his mother was so definitely eating her supper.

A few weeks later, Freddie's mother began to make preparations for Christmas.

"Isn't it a bit early, Mum?" asked Freddie. "Christmas is a long way away. We haven't even started practising carols at playgroup yet!"

"I may be rather busy nearer Christmas," explained his mother, "which reminds me, Freddie…" But Freddie had gone to watch his favourite video.

Later that week, Mum called Freddie into the kitchen.

"I'm making the Christmas pudding," she said. "The mixture is in this bowl. Now, you must give it a big stir and wish as hard as you can for something you really want. Can you do that?"

Freddie took the bowl and looked at the brown mixture. It smelled sweet and Christmassy. He was just about to put in one tiny finger for a taste, when his mother called out.

"No tasting, Freddie," she said, "or your wish may not come true, you know."

Well, that was too big a risk to take. Freddie knew exactly what he wanted to wish for – and so do you, I expect. He gave a big, big stir and wished for a baby brother to play games with. Then he had another stir and another wish just to be on the safe side.

"I've finished," he told Mum.

A couple of days later, Freddie saw his mother push away her plate of breakfast cereal. But it wasn't supper, so he didn't think anything more about it. It was true that his parents were doing a lot of whispering in the hall, but he didn't think anything about that either, because it was time for playgroup.

Freddie's father made a couple of phone calls in a quiet voice.

"Aunty May will take you to playgroup today," he said. "Mummy and I have to go into town this morning."

Freddie was surprised, but he assumed that Mum and Dad were

going to buy him his Christmas presents, even if Christmas was still a few weeks away.

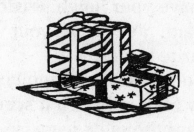

"One of those new racing games would be good," he called helpfully. That made Mum and Dad laugh out loud.

"Oh, I think we can do better than that this year!" said Dad, helping Mum on with her coat.

That morning, Freddie had a lovely time at playgroup. When it was time to go home, he found Aunty May waiting for him again.

"You can come home with me and have your lunch, Freddie," she said. "I've got all your favourite things."

Freddie went off happily with Aunty May, although it seemed as if her thoughts were somewhere else. Every time the phone rang, she jumped and ran to answer it. But it was always just someone wanting to visit her, or to sell her something to do with windows.

After an afternoon of playing, Freddie was feeling quite tired. He wondered when his Aunty would take him home to have his supper and go to bed.

"Well, you might just be going to stay with me tonight," said Aunty May, "but I'm not quite sure yet."

Not sure? But grown-ups were always sure. Freddie was just going to ask her more, when the phone rang again.

This time Aunty May talked for only a few minutes. Then she laughed and said, "That's lovely! We'll be there in twenty minutes."

Freddie found himself bundled into his coat and his aunt's car. Within seconds, they were driving along the road into town.

Aunty May stopped at a very big building. Inside, there were lots of corridors – like playschool only bigger. Freddie trotted along, holding his aunt's hand. Then, in the distance, he heard a sound that made his little heart jump for joy. It was a baby crying.

A few minutes later, Freddie was hugging his mother and his proud father and looking down at the dearest little baby brother he could have imagined.

"What's his name?" he asked.

Mum and Dad smiled and said something very strange.

"We've decided," they said, "to call him Louise."

The Magic
Trumpet

Doo, doo, de, doo! Doo, doo, de, doo! Whatever was that noise? Major Bellamy woke and sat up so quickly that he bumped his head on the bedside light.

Doo, doo, de, doo! Doo, doo, de, doo! Well, bless my soul, he thought, it sounds like a trumpet.

Major Bellamy was well used to the sound of the trumpet, having spent many years in the army overseas, but he had not heard one since his retirement. He rubbed his eyes and his ears. Had he been dreaming?

Doo, doo, de, doo! Doo, doo, de, doo! There it was again! He most definitely was *not* dreaming.

Major Bellamy pulled on his silk dressing gown with the gold tassels. He would see about this. Someone had clearly broken into his house and was making an unearthly din downstairs. But what idiot would advertise the fact that he was there? To be on the safe side, Major Bellamy picked up the sword that he used to wear with his smartest uniform. He was prepared to do battle, if he must, to defend his property and his home.

Down the stairs crept Major Bellamy. Everything seemed silent down below. Hardly daring to breathe, he pushed open the door of the dining room with his foot. A shaft of moonlight from the window lit the room almost as clearly as day.

There was no one there. Major Bellamy was a brave man. He peered under the table and behind the door. Then he looked thoughtfully at the regimental trumpet hanging on the wall. It couldn't have played by itself. Could it?

Major Bellamy shook his head.

"Too much cheese for supper," he muttered. But just then ... doo, doo, de, doo! And louder still ... DOO, DOO, DE, DOO!

Major Bellamy turned back. This time there was no doubt about it. The trumpet had played by itself. He could see that it was still trembling slightly on the wall from the effort.

Major Bellamy hesitated for a minute, but he was no coward. With one swift movement, he took the trumpet from the wall. It was slightly warm, but otherwise it felt just as it did when he took it down once a month for polishing.

Thoughtfully, Major Bellamy carried the trumpet through into the sitting room. In fact, he was concentrating so hard on the trumpet that it took him a minute to take in the scene of devastation in front of him.

The whole room looked as if a whirlwind had hit it. Books had been pulled from the shelves. The cushions had been thrown from the chairs and sofa. Pictures were hanging askew on the walls where someone had peeped behind them.

Major Bellamy felt weak at the knees, but he took a deep breath and picked up the telephone.

"Police," he said firmly. "Police, right away, please."

The old soldier replaced the telephone and sat down. He knew that he must not touch anything before the police arrived. Yet he was determined to try to work out, if he could, what had happened.

Obviously, there had been intruders. Just as clearly, the notes of the trumpet had scared them away. But what had they been looking for? And why, after hanging silently on the Major's dining room wall for nearly twenty years, had the trumpet chosen tonight to play?

Major Bellamy looked at the pictures askew on the walls. The thieves had been looking for something very small, if they thought it could be hidden on the back of a picture or, now, wait a minute, this was more like it, they had been looking for a *safe*! And if that was the case, then they were also looking for something that was so valuable they believed it would be kept in a safe.

It took Major Bellamy only a moment to work out what it could be. He had very few valuables, and he didn't for a moment think that someone would break into his house to steal a couple of medals and a pair of silver serving spoons. No, there was only one thing that was worth anything in his home, and that was the Kashmir Ruby.

Major Bellamy remembered now the darkened room in which a dying man had passed the ruby to him.

"I'm giving it to you," he had gasped, between sips of water, "because it must be owned by someone who does not care at all for its value as a jewel. If it falls into the hands of someone who wants it only for the money it is worth, it will bring him or her the worst possible bad luck for ever."

Major Bellamy had taken the jewel from the dying man, and also, yes, that was right, his trumpet – the very same one that the Major now held.

"I know now that you were not trying to protect me," said Major Bellamy to the trumpet, "but those foolish fellows who thought the jewel could bring them happiness. You have saved them from a horrible fate."

The Major left the sitting room and closed the door, pushing the doorstop away with his foot. It glowed red in the moonlight.

Aunt Bella's Umbrella

Chloe was not pleased. "Does she *have* to come?" she asked her mother, for the umpteenth time. "*Why* does she have to come?"

"She has to come because she doesn't have enough money to go on holiday, so we've invited her to stay with us for a few days. I've explained that to you, Chloe," replied her mother.

"But she wears funny clothes and she doesn't like television and she *smells* funny," said Chloe.

"Don't be ridiculous," said her mother sharply. "Aunt Bella's clothes are her own business, and she smells of lavender. It's a

lovely perfume. I can't think why you're getting in such a state about this."

Chloe didn't say anything. She knew that her mother wouldn't have any sympathy if she did tell her the real reason. Aunt Bella was going to have to sleep in *her* room, in the bed her sister slept in when she wasn't away on a school trip. When the two girls were together, they had a lovely time, giggling and whispering after the lights were out. Even when Hannah wasn't there, Chloe could have fun creeping out of bed and playing quietly with some of her toys. But Aunt

Bella was a different matter entirely. Chloe was pretty sure *she* wouldn't want to play games. And what if ... what a horrible thought! What if she snored?

Aunt Bella arrived by train that afternoon. Chloe's Dad went to collect her from the station. When they reached home, Aunt Bella had only a battered old suitcase and a bright red umbrella with her. She insisted on putting both of these in Chloe's room, although Chloe's Mum tried hard to get her to leave her umbrella in the hall.

"Oh, no," said Aunt Bella. "This old umbrella comes with me."

That night, Aunt Bella decided to go to bed at the same time as Chloe, which was quite early.

"I'm tired from the journey," she said, "and this way, I won't wake you up when I come in, will I, sweetheart?"

Chloe had hoped to be fast asleep when Aunt Bella went to bed, so that she didn't know anything about it, but she smiled politely and showed her aunt where her towels were and how the bedside light worked.

When Aunt Bella emerged from the bathroom, she was wearing an extraordinary purple dressing gown and curlers in her hair.

Chloe had to stuff her sheets in her mouth to stop herself laughing out loud.

Chloe's mother put her head round the door and smiled as she said, "Goodnight, girls!"

Chloe lay awake in the darkness, listening hard. Could she hear just the tiniest little bit of snoring?

"No, she doesn't snore," said a voice from the other side of the room in a friendly way.

"Oh! I didn't say it out loud, did I?" asked Chloe, before she had time to think.

"No, of course not," replied her aunt, in quite a different kind of voice, "but sometimes he can tell what you're thinking."

"Who can?" asked Chloe.

"My umbrella, of course. He's magic and helps me to do all kinds of things."

Chloe thought for a moment.

"It's true," said the umbrella. "She's not completely batty."

"Oh, I'm sorry," gasped Chloe. "I didn't mean to think that. It just popped into my head."

"Don't worry," said Aunt Bella. "But you just behave yourself, umbrella! Just be a little bit more careful about what you say."

"All right," said the umbrella, "but I should just mention that this little girl thinks that your dressing gown is pretty funny as well, you know."

"Well, she's entitled to her opinion," said Aunt Bella. "Now, where shall we go tonight, umbrella?"

"I was wondering about a trip to Venice," said the umbrella carelessly. "I've heard it's not too crowded at this time of year."

"Lovely," said Aunt Bella. "Now, Chloe, shut your eyes and think about umbrellas."

Chloe couldn't believe this was happening, but she did as she was told. She imagined umbrellas in all kinds of colours. They began to whirl about before her eyes, faster and faster.

"Now open your eyes," said Aunt Bella. Chloe found herself in a little boat, gliding along a canal between tall buildings. In front of her was her aunt, holding her umbrella over her head like a parasol.

"This is Venice," said Aunt Bella. "It's beautiful, isn't it?"

"But where is it?" asked Chloe. "It doesn't look like anywhere I know at all."

"It's in a country called Italy," explained Aunt Bella, "a long, long way from your home. Do you like it?"

"I'd like one of those ice creams over there," replied Chloe. She had just spotted a man with a little stall on one side of the canal.

Five minutes later, Chloe had her mouth full of the tastiest ice cream she had ever eaten. But Aunt Bella's umbrella began to flutter above her head.

"Oops a daisy," said Aunt Bella. "It looks as though it's time to go home. Shut your eyes, Chloe."

The next minute, Chloe found herself back in her own little bed.

"Time to sleep, now," said Aunt Bella. "We can go travelling again tomorrow night, if you like."

Chloe could hardly count the wonderful places she visited over the next few nights, but all too soon it was time for Aunt Bella to go home.

"You were a good girl to share your room," said Chloe's mother, as they waved Aunt Bella off in the train. "She has so few chances to get away, I felt we had to help."

"I'm not so sure about that," said Chloe quietly, "but I'm very glad you invited her *here*. And her umbrella."

Chloe's mother wasn't sure she had heard her daughter properly. She couldn't mind about an umbrella, could she?

The
Contrary
Princess

Once upon a time there was a Princess who was very cross and difficult. She disagreed with everything that was said to her, just for the sake of it. And because she was a Princess, everyone agreed with her, however silly she was being.

You wouldn't believe how annoying the Princess could be. Suppose someone came to visit her and said, "That is a beautiful dress you are wearing, Your Highness." The Princess would immediately reply, "This is an awful, ugly dress. I can't bear the sight of it. I shall take it off at once." If someone praised a clump of flowers in the royal garden, she would at once declare that they were common and uninteresting, and she would order the gardeners to dig them up at once.

This ridiculous state of affairs went on for some time, until one day a fairy happened to be passing when the Princess was being particularly contrary. (As a matter of fact, it wouldn't have made very much difference when the fairy had flown by, as the Princess was always the same.)

As the fairy flew past, she heard the Princess declare, "It doesn't matter what you say,

Father, you are sure to be wrong, and I shall be right." Now, apart from the fact that this was not at all a nice way to speak to the King, it was also a really very silly thing to say. No one is right all the time. And no one is wrong all the time for that matter.

"Very well," said the fairy, "if you must be so contrary, I will make sure that everything you say is exactly the opposite of what you mean – always." She said a quick spell, and the deed was done.

That evening, a maid servant brought the Princess her supper. "The cook has asked me to tell you that the soup is particularly delicious today," she said.

The Princess tasted a spoonful. "Yes," she said, "this is the most delicious soup I have ever tasted."

The maid servant almost dropped her tray in amazement. Had she heard correctly? Had the Princess actually liked something?

The Princess was just as amazed. That hadn't been what she had meant to say at all – far from it. But the maid was smiling and making an extra low curtsey, instead of flouncing off as she often did.

Next morning, the King came to his daughter and suggested that they go riding together.

"That would be delightful," said the Princess, much to her own amazement. The King was so touched that he had tears in his eyes. It was a very, very long time since his daughter had shown any kindness towards a member of her own family.

In fact, the King and the Princess spent a very pleasant morning. The Princess agreed that the countryside was beautiful and her father's horse was spirited. She confessed that the castle looked very handsome

on its hill and that, yes, perhaps it was time she considered finding a Prince and setting up a home of her own.

The King was amazed and delighted. His daughter seemed to be growing up at last, and he could not have been more pleased that she was seriously considering settling down.

The Princess, on the other hand, was confused and a little frightened. Not one of the nice things she had said had been in her mind before they popped out of her mouth. And as for getting married, nothing was further from her thoughts! But all the same, it was rather touching to see her father looking so happy.

The King lost no time in setting about finding a husband for his precious daughter. All the Princes from nearby lands were invited to a grand ball at the palace.

On the evening of the ball, the Princess wore her most magnificent dress. She looked down from the balcony at all the young men who had gathered to pay court to her and found that she despised them all. Yet, when one of them asked whether she would like to dance, she found herself telling him that nothing could be more charming.

Altogether, the more horrible the Princess wanted to be, the more friendly and pleasant she found herself seeming. It was intensely annoying.

Now one Prince had been watching the Princess very closely. When she withdrew to a nearby room for a moment to catch her breath, he slipped in behind her.

"Your Highness," he said, gently. "Can you really be charmed by so many different Princes? Are you not deceiving us all?"

The Princess looked at him gratefully, as if to say, "Yes, you are right, so right!" but out of her

mouth came the words, "No, Sir,
I find you all equally delightful."

Then the Prince told the
Princess what he really thought.
"I believe that you have been
bewitched, Your Highness," he
said. "If you will allow me, I can
lift the spell and return you to
yourself."

"Please don't," said the Princess,
but her eyes said otherwise.

The Prince stepped forward
and kissed the Princess, which at
once broke the fairy's spell.

"Forgive me," said the Prince.
"It was the only way to undo the
magic. Now you may be as
horrid to me as you like."

But after a month of having her nasty comments changed to nice ones, the Princess suddenly found that what she wanted to say more than anything else was the truth.

"Sir," she said, "You told me that I was bewitched before, but now I believe you have bewitched me again." And she kissed the Prince, to show him exactly what she meant.

The Prince and the Princess have been married for a year now. The Princess always says exactly what she means, and so does the Prince. You have only to look at them to see that this suits them very well indeed.

Wise
Wishes

Every day, we make wishes. "I wish the sun would shine," we say, when we want to have a picnic. "I wish it would rain," we say, when we want to avoid going for a long walk with an energetic uncle.

If you think about it, you will realise that everyone simply cannot have all their wishes come true all the time. After all, your energetic uncle is probably wishing for sunshine, just as you are wishing for rain.

Now wishes are magical things, and magic needs to be taken very seriously indeed. It can do wonderful things, and it can do terrible things. You need to be very careful what you wish for.

Once upon a time, there was a little boy. When he watched his elder brothers playing together, he wanted so much to join in. But his brothers laughed. "You're much too young to play with us," they said.

So the little boy shut his eyes and wished with all his heart. "I wish I could be older," he said, and pretty soon, he was.

A few years later, the boy's brothers began to get married. The boy met a lovely girl who was as pretty as she was clever. "Will you be my wife?" he asked.

But the pretty girl just laughed. "You're much too young to be married," she said.

Once again, the boy shut his eyes and made his wish. "I wish I could be older," he said, and very soon, he was.

The boy married the pretty girl and settled down. He wanted to earn lots of money for his wife and growing family, so he went to his employer and asked to be made a partner in the company.

"My boy," laughed his boss, "you're much too young to be made a partner."

The boy – who was a man now – closed his eyes and wished from the bottom of his heart. "I wish I could be older," he said, and in the twinkling of an eye, he was.

The man became a partner in his company and did well. His children grew up and left home.

Then the man began to be tired of working every day. He went to the other partners and said, "I have been thinking about the path my life has taken, and I should like to retire very soon."

But the other partners laughed. "You're much too young to retire," they said. "We need you here."

Then the man shut his eyes and wished with all his power. "I wish I could be older," he said, and in no time at all, he was.

So the man retired from his business and enjoyed playing with his grandchildren. But the day came when they ran away from him, laughing, and called, "You can't catch us, Grandpa. You're much too old!"

It was true. Then the man sat down, for he was feeling tired, and he wished harder than he had ever wished in his life. "I wish," he said, "I could be younger."

It is a strange thing that all the other wishes he had ever made came true. But his last wish never did.

If I could wish one thing for you, dear reader, it is that you should take more care with your own wishes than that poor man.

Are there many kinds of wishes?
No, there are only two:
Those that bring us what we wish
And those that never do.

The
Apple Spell

Once there was a little girl who loved apples more than anything else in the world. She would have eaten apples for breakfast, lunch and supper if her mother had let her.

She was rather a greedy little girl, too. She couldn't help feeling that every apple someone else ate was an apple she couldn't eat herself! When you think of all the apples there are in the world, that was really very silly, wasn't it?

One day when she was out walking, the little girl, whose name was Bessie, saw an old lady, sitting by the side of the road. Next to her was a basket of beautiful apples.

"Hello, sweetheart," said the old lady in a quavering voice, "can you help me, please?"

Bessie slowly went over to the old lady. She felt annoyed that her walk had been interrupted.

"I sat down here for a moment for a rest," explained the old lady, "and I can't persuade my poor old legs to get up again.

I just need a bit of a heave-ho from a big, strong girl like you."

Bessie's eyes grew brighter as she saw the big basket of apples, and she had an idea.

"I'll help you," she said, "if you will give me one of your apples."

Now the old lady would have offered the little girl an apple for her kindness, but being asked for something is rather different.

"And if I don't give you an apple?" asked the old lady, looking sharply at Bessie. "I just want to be sure I understand."

Bessie blinked. She hadn't really thought that far. She wasn't really an unpleasant girl, but now that she thought about it, a bargain was a bargain.

"Well, if you don't" she said, "I suppose I shall leave you here."

"I see," said the old lady. "Very well, my dear. I will give you an apple when you have helped me to my feet." And she stretched out her gnarled old hands.

Bessie seized the old woman and gave a big pull.

"Heave-ho!" chuckled the old lady, and she hopped so nimbly to her feet that Bessie was surprised she had needed help.

"Well, thank you very much, my dear," said the old lady cheerfully. "Goodbye!"

She picked up her basket and set off down the road.

"Just a minute," cried Bessie loudly. "What about my apple?"

The old lady paused. "I was just giving you one last chance," she said under her breath, holding out the basket.

Bessie picked the rosiest, roundest apple she could see. It looked so delicious that she immediately took a huge bite.

"Goodbye again!" called the old lady.

"Ooooeye!" cried Bessie.

"You shouldn't talk with your mouth full, dear," said the old lady, smiling.

"I aah ehh iii oww o iii oww!" said Bessie.

The old lady knew perfectly well what she was trying to say. When Bessie took a huge bite of the apple, it had become stuck in her mouth. She could neither munch through it nor pull her teeth out of it. It was really a most *un*glamorous situation to be in!

"I should have thought, my dear," said the old lady, "that you would be happy to be *always* eating something you are so very fond of." And she turned away.

You may have guessed by now that the old lady had magic

powers. A tiny spell was making Bessie very, very uncomfortable.

What if she could never speak again? What if she could never eat anything else ever again? Bessie's eyes filled with tears.

The old lady looked thoughtful for a moment. She could see that the little girl really was feeling sorry for herself – and perhaps she was feeling a little bit sorry about her behaviour too. She said a few words under her breath, and Bessie's apple fell to the ground.

"I'm sorry," sobbed Bessie. "I know I was greedy."

The old lady smiled gently. "Sometimes unpleasant things can teach us a great deal about ourselves," she said. "Now this time, I really will say goodbye, my dear."

When Bessie looked up, the old lady had vanished!

Bessie hurried home, where her mother was preparing supper for the family.

"I'm glad you're here, Bessie," she said. "Supper is nearly ready. I've made your favourite dessert, too. Apple pie!"

Bessie felt a little faint. Somehow she felt that she couldn't face another apple.

You know, that little girl has been a much nicer person recently. She helps at home and tries very hard to think about other people and not about what *she* wants all the time.

Oh, and what is her favourite food in all the world? Why, bananas, of course!

Goodnight, Little Goblin

There was once a little goblin called Bramble. He was a very good little goblin in *almost* every way. He played nicely with his little sister, even when she sat on his racing car and squashed it. He ate up all his dinner, even when it was rice pudding. He even helped his mother with the washing up ... sometimes. But there was one thing that Bramble would not do. He would not go to bed when his mother told him it was time.

Bramble's parents had tried everything to persuade their son to go to bed. They had tried threatening him with rice

pudding for a week. They had
tried rewarding him with no rice
pudding for two weeks. They had
even decorated his bedroom
with cars and aeroplanes, so that
Bramble couldn't wait to go into
his bedroom at night.

But being in his bedroom
didn't mean that Bramble was in
his bed, and it certainly didn't
mean that he was asleep. There
never was a goblin boy with so
many excuses for staying awake.

"Why aren't you asleep,
Bramble?" his mother would ask,
peeping around the door.

"It's much too light in here,"
Bramble would reply. "The stars

are shining right into my room.
Look! No one could sleep in all
this starlight."

"I see," said his mother, and
she went downstairs. The next
day, Bramble's mother made him
extra-thick curtains, so that not
one drop of starlight shone into
his room. But the next night,
when she peeped round the
door, Bramble was wide awake
as usual.

"What is it now, Bramble?" she
asked wearily.

"I'm too hot," said Bramble, "with those thick curtains over the window, and anyway, I can't see to play now."

"You're not supposed to be playing!" cried his mother. "It's night time, Bramble, when all little goblins should be in bed and fast asleep. Don't let me find you awake again."

But Bramble just did not want to sleep. There were too many interesting things to do to waste time sleeping.

When Bramble's parents were at their wits' ends, his Great Uncle Gorse came to stay. Great Uncle Gorse was a rather stern old goblin. His great niece and great nephew were a little bit afraid of him, because they had once overheard their mother saying that the old man knew quite a lot about magic. Now, when he peered at them over his spectacles, he looked too ordinary to be able to do magic.

Bramble rather thought that magic was a made-up thing in any case. "I think it only happened in olden times and in stories," he told his sister. "There isn't any magic around today."

But that was where Bramble was quite, quite wrong. Great Uncle Gorse certainly did know some magic. In fact, he knew more than almost any other living goblin.

It was not long before Great Uncle Gorse found out about Bramble's unwillingness to sleep.

"That's ridiculous," he told Bramble's mother. "What have you tried?"

"Everything," she sighed.

"Have you tried … a little … well, of the *old* ways, my dear?"

"You mean m-m-m-magic?" gasped his niece. "Oh, I don't think that would be a good idea. Bramble is very young, you know, and magic is such dangerous stuff."

"I promise you that no harm will come to the boy," said the old goblin. "Now, this is what I suggest…"

The next night, Bramble went to bed as usual. But did he go to sleep? Oh no! First he got out of bed and played with his cars for a while. (His mother came in twice to plead with him to go to sleep during this time.) Then he pretended to be a spaceman and jumped across his bed as though he was on the moon. (His mother came in once more while this was going on.) Being a spaceman made Bramble think about explorers, so he began an expedition to find out what was under his bed. (His mother came in again while he was doing this and was nearly frightened out of her wits when she couldn't see Bramble *anywhere*.)

By the time Bramble had finished his under-bed exploration, and found several toys that he had completely forgotten about, the whole house was quiet. His mother and father and Great Uncle Gorse had all gone to bed.

Bramble made himself a sandwich and read an interesting book about pirates, using his torch under the bedclothes.

After that, even Bramble was beginning to feel rather sleepy. Perhaps it was time for a quick snooze after all. But Bramble quickly found a very strange thing. He couldn't close his eyes!

"How horrible!" you will say. "The poor boy's eyeballs will shrivel up!" Perhaps I have given the wrong impression. It wasn't actually that Bramble couldn't close his eyes. He simply couldn't *keep* them closed. He could blink, but when he tried to keep his eyes shut, they just bounced open again.

At first, Bramble wasn't too worried, but the longer this

happened, the more he found that the one thing he really wanted to do was to go to sleep. He tried everything he could think of, but the fact of the matter is that it is very difficult indeed to go to sleep with your eyes open.

Before long, Bramble saw the pink light of dawn creeping through his window. Morning was coming, and he hadn't had a single wink of sleep.

There were lots of interesting things happening that day, but Bramble didn't really feel like any of them. He played in the goblin goal in an elves *v.* goblins football match and let in twelve goals. He did an experiment in his science lesson and nearly set fire to the classroom. When it was time to go home, he was almost run over by a goblin cart because he was too tired to concentrate when he crossed the road outside the school. It really was one of the most dreadful days he had ever known.

That evening at supper, Bramble could hardly keep his eyes open, although, of course, he couldn't keep them shut, either. Each time he looked up, he could see Great Uncle Gorse peering at him through his spectacles with a strange expression on his face.

"What would you like to do now more than anything else in the world?" the old goblin asked his great nephew.

"Oh, Great Uncle Gorse," cried Bramble, "I just want to go to bed!"

One smile from Great Uncle Gorse lifted the spell, and Bramble was asleep before his head hit the pillow.

I have heard that he now goes to sleep as well as any little boy in Goblinville. And if he ever goes back to his old ways, Great Uncle Gorse has an open invitation to come to stay...

The Elf Who Couldn't Spell

Once upon a time, there was a little elf who would *not* pay attention at school. He would look out of the window, or draw pictures in his book, or simply float away in a world of his own, imagining what it would be like to be a grown-up elf.

As you know, it is always very important to listen carefully during lessons. At any moment, you may learn something that will be useful to you five minutes later or for the rest of your life.

It is a great pity that Elderberry Elf was not paying attention one Tuesday morning last autumn when Mrs Maple was teaching one of her interesting classes in Elementary Magic.

"Now remember," she said, "these words must *always* be used at the end of each spell. If they are not, then you will not be able to undo the spell. Are you listening, Elderberry?"

"Yes, Mrs Maple," said the little elf. "We must always use those words at the end of a spell, so that we can undo it if we want to."

"Good," said Mrs Maple. "If there is one thing you must remember from everything I teach you this year, it is that."

Well, it *sounded* as though Elderberry understood, and in a way he did, but there was one big problem. *He couldn't remember what "those words" were!* Elderberry knew that he *should* ask his teacher, but he couldn't quite bring himself to admit he had not been listening. And the longer he left it, the harder it became to ask the question. From time to time, the little elf worried about those words he did not know, but usually he tried not to think about it.

Now, I'm sure you're imagining that something dreadful happened to Elderberry. Did he turn himself into a cabbage and have to stay like that? Did he take a magic trip to Peru, and is he still there? Well, no. What Elderberry did was to try out a little magic to make him forget all the spells he had learnt. This is a useful spell to use on evil wizards, of course, but it is better to practise on yourself first … if you remember "those words" so that you can reverse it.

The result is that Elderberry now cannot do any magic at all. This sometimes makes him sad, but I think that we are all much, much safer that way. If you see Elderberry, you won't tell him any of *your* magic, will you?

The
Elegant Elf

Once upon a time, there was an elf who cared for nothing but clothes. Only the finest were good enough for him. If everyone else had five buttons on their jackets, he had six – and they were gold ones, of course. When cloaks were in fashion, the elegant elf's cloak was so long that there was hardly room for it in his cottage.

In fact, most of the rooms in his home were filled with clothes, but the elegant elf didn't mind that. He wanted to keep an eye on his precious jackets and waistcoats, not to mention his socks and knickerbockers!

The elegant elf was sure that nobody could take as much care with his clothes as he liked, so he washed and ironed them himself, paying careful attention to every velvet ruffle and every silken pleat.

It was not surprising that the elegant elf had very little time for anything other than his clothes. In the morning, it took him at least an hour to decide what to wear. First he would look out of the window to see what the weather was like. On a rainy day, he would never go outside, in case his silk stockings got splashed. On a snowy day, he

liked to show off his coat made
of thistledown, with its wool
lining, but he was worried about
his hat getting damp, so he only
went out when the snow was
sparkling underfoot, not falling
from the sky. On a sunny day, the
elf had an even bigger problem.
He liked to wear as many clothes
as possible, so that all the other
elves could admire them, but
that meant he was terribly hot!

Even when he had decided
which clothes to wear, it took the
elf another hour to get dressed.
After all, it takes time to do up
one hundred and seventy-two
tiny buttons on a satin waistcoat!

The moment of the day that the elf liked best was when he stood in front of the mirror, just before he set off for his walk through the village. His clothes were perfect. Not a speck of dust or a smear of mud could be seen. The elegant elf would sigh with happiness as he admired himself.

Strangely enough, the elf did not know what the other elves thought as they saw him walk slowly down the street. He was sure that they were all admiring him, wishing they had clothes like his, but he never turned his head to make sure, in case it made his hat tip to one side!

In fact, the other elves thought he was very, very silly.

"Did you see him today?" asked Twinkletoes in the bakery one morning. "He was wearing purple boots with gold tassels. Imagine!"

"That's nothing," said Acorn. "Yesterday he had a hat shaped like a dandelion. It looked ridiculous."

"I've never talked to him," said Mayflower, "but I've heard that he's a very stuck-up kind of elf. He thinks he's better than the rest of us."

"I don't think any of us have ever talked to him," agreed

Twinkletoes, "but I'm sure it's true that he's not a very nice elf. It's just as well that he keeps himself to himself."

And that was the way things stayed. No one spoke to the elegant elf and he spoke to no one. The other elves believed that he thought himself too good for them, while he was sure that they all admired him so much that they were afraid to speak to him.

Things might have stayed like that for a very long time – perhaps for ever – if it hadn't been for the Great Storm of Elftown. It happened one autumn day, when the last brown leaves

were swirling from the trees.
First a little breeze began to
blow, and elves going about their
business turned their collars up.
Then dark clouds began to
gather overhead, and elves with
washing drying outside hurried
out to take it in.

Gradually, the wind grew
fiercer. No one was too worried
when old Farmer Fern's fence
blew down, because it always
had been rather rickety. But
when his hen house came flying
down the high street, elves locked
their windows and doors and
huddled closer to the fire. They
had never seen such a storm.

The wind blew and blew, and just when everyone thought that nothing worse could happen, the rain began. It didn't fall in drops. It fell in sheets, as though someone up in the sky was emptying a whole bathtub over Elftown. All the elves who were crouching in their warm houses felt very glad to be indoors, even if a few drops were coming through the roof. They peered out of their windows at the wild weather and hoped that their gardens would not be completely washed away.

The elegant elf, too, was looking out of his window. He

wasn't too worried about the storm but he was worried about how he would get his washing dry. It was sitting in a basket in the kitchen, and he felt sure that his silk knickerbockers would be terribly creased if they were left much longer.

But as the elegant elf gazed anxiously at the sky, he noticed a movement in the street. There in the wind and weather, an elf mother and her little boy were struggling along. Their clothes were wet and cold, and at every second it seemed that the gale would blow them away. They had been in the woods, gathering berries, when the storm began, and were trying desperately to reach their home.

The other elves saw them too, from their cosy homes.

"I wish I could help them," said Mayflower, "but the weather is just too bad."

"Those poor elves," said Twinkletoes sadly. "I'd love to rescue them, but there's no point in three of us being washed away and never seen again."

"They shouldn't have been out so far from home on a day like this," said Acorn. "Some elves don't have the sense they were born with."

The elegant elf didn't say any of those things. He didn't shake his head, or turn his back, or settle down by his fire. He opened his front door and rushed out into the rain, calling out to the half-drowned elves.

Now the elegant elf didn't think for one minute about the golden fringe on his coat or the velvet decorations on his hat, although all of them were ruined in ten seconds flat. He simply ran towards the mother and child, scooped them up under his coat, and carried them back to his cottage, struggling against the wind and rain at every step.

"Well!" cried Twinkletoes, who had seen everything. "Who would have guessed it?"

"I wouldn't have believed it," cried Mayflower, "if I hadn't seen it with my own eyes."

Even Acorn cleared his throat and muttered, "Ahem ... perhaps I've misjudged that elf. He must be good hearted after all."

If you spend a morning in Elftown today, you could almost believe that nothing has changed. The elegant elf still spends all his time thinking about his clothes. He still takes two hours to get ready in the morning. The other elves still

don't talk to him or invite him to
their houses. But when he walks
down the village street each
morning, showing off his clothes,
every single elf on the street
puts down his shopping and,
with a loud cheer, claps his
hands and stamps his feet.
Sometimes the applause can be
heard all the way to Goblinville.

Well, the town elves are happy
because they feel that they have
let him know how they feel about
his brave rescue. And the elegant
elf is happier still, because he is
sure that those elves have seen
the error of their ways at last and
are finally cheering ... his clothes.

Mayflower's
Carrots

Mayflower was a very busy little elf. He had lots of hobbies and was always taking up new ones. As a result, his spare bedroom was full of half-finished projects. There was a model aeroplane with one wing, a cane chair with half a seat, a tapestry with one corner finished, and a pile of newspapers with a heavy weight on top. Between the newspapers were the pressed flowers that Mayflower had collected with great enthusiasm one summer, but Mayflower's wife had forgotten about that and regularly used the papers for lighting the fire.

One afternoon, Mayflower went to visit his old friend Acorn. As he sat in front of the fire, sipping a cup of dandelion tea, the curious elf was surprised to see some brightly coloured rosettes in pride of place above the older elf's fireplace.

"What are those, Acorn?" asked Mayflower, getting up to take a closer look.

"Aha!" smiled Acorn proudly. "Those are my rosettes for winning prizes at last year's Grand Fruit and Vegetable Show in Goblinville. They hold one every summer, you know, but I had never entered until last year."

"And yet you won so many prizes," said Mayflower in surprise. "What about the goblins? Didn't they win anything?"

"I'm afraid those goblins don't know much about gardening," said Acorn. "Oh, they can grow a good toadstool, I'm not denying it, but when it comes to parsnips and beans and potatoes, they don't have a clue!"

Mayflower was very thoughtful as he made his way home that day. He had never had much success with gardening in the past. There had been those extra special daisies that he had sent away for. Every one of them

shrivelled and died within weeks.
It may partly have been due to the
fact that Mayflower almost always
forgot to water them, of course.

Then there had been his
doomed attempt to grow cacti.

"You can't go wrong, old chap,"
Twinkletoes had told him. "They
need hardly any water at all."

So Mayflower had bought ten
different kinds of cactus, each one
more prickly than the one before.
He was very careful not to water
them too little or too much, but
month after month passed and
still they did not flower.

"It might take years," said
Twinkletoes, when Mayflower

complained. "Are you giving them enough sunlight?"

In fact, the cacti were in rather a dark corner, so Mayflower brought them out on to the windowsill, where the sun could reach them. Unfortunately, it was winter, and the sun only peeped out from behind the clouds for a few minutes every day.

"These poor cacti are freezing to death," said Mayflower to his wife. "No wonder they're not flowering." A sensible elf would have waited until spring to see what would happen, but Mayflower, as always, was impatient. He took the cacti and popped them in the oven for a few minutes.

I'm sure I don't need to tell you what happened. Mayflower turned away for a few seconds to make himself a cup of tea. Then he searched for some biscuits in the cupboards. Then he knocked his tea over by mistake and had to start again. By the time the silly elf turned back to rescue his cacti, they were well and truly cooked.

Mayflower vowed that he would never have anything to do with gardening again.

But now Acorn's prizes had set him thinking. Some rosettes above his fireplace would certainly look very fine.

"Now, what did Acorn say he had grown?" Mayflower asked himself. "It was parsnips and beans and potatoes. I must try something else, so that I don't have to compete with Acorn. It will be easy to beat those stupid old goblins."

That night, as he sat down to supper, Mayflower asked his wife to tell him what her favourite vegetables were.

"Oh, I love tomatoes," said Cowslip, "and I'm very fond of carrots too. But why are you asking, Mayflower?"

"Oh, no reason," replied Mayflower airily.

Cowslip gave her husband a suspicious look. She knew that his ideas usually ended in disaster and she was afraid that this would be another one.

"I simply thought that I would try my hand at vegetable growing," her husband explained. It seemed wiser not to mention the Grand Fruit and Vegetable Show yet, just in case the vegetables were not a great success.

Cowslip thought for a moment. She really couldn't see how things could go badly wrong, and it would be nice to have some really fresh vegetables for a change.

Over the next few weeks, Mayflower worked very hard. No one could say that the elf was not making every effort to do things the right way. He found a book in the Elf and Goblin Visiting Library about vegetable growing and read everything it said on Preparing the Soil. For a whole week he dug and forked and raked in the back garden, until he had a little plot that looked as trim and neat as the one he had glimpsed through Acorn's window. Then he set off to Goblinville to buy his seed.

The shops in Goblinville are much bigger than those in Elftown. Mayflower visited several before he found that the ironmonger's also sold vegetable seed. But what a lot of different packets there were to choose from! And they all had such pretty pictures on the front.

Mayflower looked at the carrot packets first. Sweet and Small, Tasty and Tiny, and Mini Mouthful were good names for carrots, but they didn't sound quite right for a vegetable show. Mayflower had a feeling that vegetables needed to be big if they were to win prizes.

The eager elf was just beginning to feel discouraged when he spotted a slightly larger packet at the back of the rack. It looked rather old and dusty, but the name in big, old-fashioned letters on the front made Mayflower very happy.

"GOBLIN'S ORANGE GIANT," he read, "that's the one for me, no doubt about it."

Mayflower was so pleased with his discovery that he forgot all about the tomatoes. He hurried home with his packet and sat down to read the instructions.

Now it may be that you don't know very much about goblin gardening, and Mayflower was just the same. Acorn was wrong when he said that goblins could not grow fine vegetables. In fact, goblins can grow anything they want to, because they use magic. As magic is not allowed in the Grand Fruit and Vegetable Show, very few goblins bother to use non-magical methods and enter the show.

Some elves are very good at magic, too, but it may not surprise you to learn that Mayflower had never managed to pass his First Proficiency Badge at school. And evening classes since then hadn't helped very much either.

That is why, when Mayflower read the instructions on the packet, he didn't realize that magic was involved. He thought that everyone recited a few words over their carrot seed once it was in the ground. If he had known that it was magic, I think that even Mayflower would not have been silly enough to try it. But on the other hand...

So, on the day following a new moon, as the packet advised, Mayflower stood in his garden, looking down at one neat row of carrot seed and said:

Hobble gobble, wind blow,
Rain fall and carrots grow.
Hobble gobble, sun shine,
Dig them up and they'll be fine.

I must warn you now, if you ever decide to grow carrots, don't *ever* say that rhyme within their hearing. The results could be too disastrous to think about.

Poor Mayflower! Perhaps it was a pity that the weather just then decided to be very changeable. That night, the wind blew and the rain came down. In the morning, the sun shone over the whole of Elftown … but not into Mayflower's bedroom, which was as dark as if it were the middle of the night.

I expect you can guess what had happened. Overnight, the whole row of carrots had grown … and grown … and GROWN! Their tops were covering Mayflower's bedroom window, so that not a twinkle of sunshine could peep through. And the orange roots of the carrots, appearing through the soil, were so big that they filled the whole garden.

If it had been left to Mayflower, it might have been ages before the problem was discovered. He just kept opening his eyes and saying, "Oh, it's still night. I can have another little sleep." This might have gone on all day, but Cowslip knew at once that something was wrong. Apart from anything else, there was a strong smell of *carrot* all through the house!

"I'll get to the bottom of this," she said, and she stormed out of the front door in her dressing gown. When she saw the giant carrots, poor Cowslip sat down and laughed until the tears ran down her face. It wasn't really funny to have a garden full of giant carrots, but somehow she couldn't help herself.

"Come out here, Mayflower!" she called. "Look at your gardening. It's been ... well ... rather too successful!"

For one brief moment, Mayflower's spirits soared when he saw the giant carrots.

"They will win a prize for sure," he cried happily. "Poor old Acorn can't beat this!"

"What prize?" asked Cowslip. "And what's it got to do with Acorn? Now, Mayflower, tell me everything."

And that's what Mayflower did.

"You are a noodle, Mayflower," said Cowslip. "You can't win a prize with these carrots. How on earth do you think you are going to dig them up?"

Mayflower's face fell. "Perhaps if I asked some friends to help…" he began hopefully.

"And how do you think you are going to take them to Goblinville?" asked Cowslip.

"Oh … er … well…" Mayflower could not think of anything to say at all. "What are we going to do?" he asked in a small voice, after a long silence.

"There is only one thing we can do," said Cowslip firmly. "We must go and ask my uncle the goblin for help. I don't like doing it, because he doesn't have a very high opinion of elves anyway, but in this situation, we have no other choice, I'm afraid."

So this time it was Cowslip who set off for Goblinville, having given Mayflower strict instructions about several important jobs that needed doing inside the house.

Cowslip spent a long time with her uncle. He laughed so hard when he heard the story that he could hardly speak for an hour or so. When at last he could talk without giggling, he wrote down a few important words for his niece on a piece of paper.

That evening, Cowslip and Mayflower stood in a tiny corner of the garden as the carrots towered over them. Cowslip read from her piece of paper:

Hobble gobble, wind blow,
Rain fall and carrots go.
Hobble gobble, sun shine,
Go to bed and you'll be fine.

When he woke in the morning, Mayflower hardly dared to open his eyes. But when he did so, he saw golden sunshine pouring into the bedroom. Down in the garden, there was not a carrot to be seen, just some rather large holes and a slightly startled rabbit.

Mayflower began to feel very much better. When he thought about it, his gardening had been quite a success. The only trouble was that it had been *too much* of a success. Perhaps if he didn't try quite so hard next time…

Cowslip came down to breakfast to find her husband pulling on his boots, his travelling hat by his side. She gave him one very serious look.

"I thought I'd go into Goblinville," said Mayflower, "to buy some tomato seed. You said how much you liked tomatoes. This time I'd make sure I didn't…"

Mayflower's voice trailed off as he saw the expression on Cowslip's face.

"Or…" he said quickly, "I might just go in and buy some tomatoes instead. How would that be?"

"That would be much, much better," said Cowslip. And it was.

The Elf
in the
Tree

Once there was an elf who really hated housework. He hated tidying up and dusting and sweeping and polishing. Most of all, he hated washing up. All those bubbles got up his rather long nose and made him sneeze. And the water made his cuffs soggy.

"Why don't you do it all just once a week?" suggested one friend. "Then it would be over and done with for another thirteen days." (Elf weeks are not quite the same as ours, but it would take too long to explain why. Months are different too, but they don't come into this story, so it doesn't matter. And as for elf clocks…)

Well, Hollyhock (for that was his name) thought that the once-a-week idea was an excellent one. The only trouble was that he never could decide which day would be the best to begin. Each morning when he woke up he thought, "Oh no, I couldn't face it today." So the dust kept settling and the dishes kept piling up in the sink.

What with one thing and another, the house began to be rather *smelly*. Hollyhock grew so used to it that he didn't really mind very much, but he did notice that most of his friends had stopped coming to see him, and he wondered why.

"Er, Tumbledown," he said one day. "Is there ... is there ... anything I should know about? I mean elves used to be dropping in every day, but now I hardly see anyone from one week to the next."

Now it was well known that Tumbledown had no sense of smell at all, ever since he had put his head into a pepper mine and sneezed so hard that his ears almost fell off. But there was nothing wrong with Tumbledown's ears now, and he had heard the other elves complaining about Hollyhock's house. Still, it was a delicate matter, and he didn't quite know how to begin.

"I believe, my old friend, that it's a matter of … well … *odour*," he said hesitantly.

"What?" asked Hollyhock. "What's *odour*?"

"It's … well … it's a certain lack of … er … *fragrance*," stuttered Tumbledown, his face growing red.

"I still don't understand what you're talking about," replied his friend. "What is it that my house doesn't have?"

"To put it plainly," replied Tumbledown, "your house doesn't have a pleasant *aroma*."

Hollyhook looked blank. "I still haven't got the faintest idea what you mean," he said. "Please tell me

427

in simple words, Tumbledown. If you won't tell me the truth, who can I ask?"

Then Tumbledown took pity on his friend. Putting an arm across the young elf's shoulder, he said kindly, "My boy, your house *smells*. That's why no one comes to visit you any more. It doesn't worry me, since my visit to the pepper mine, but it upsets the other elves a good deal."

Hollyhook went very pink and looked around him. The house was in a terrible state. Cobwebs hung across the windows and dust lay thick on the table. There was a half-eaten sandwich on the chair

and a mouldy apple on the shelf.
And yes, even he had to admit it,
there was a strange and not very
pleasant smell about the place.

Tumbledown looked at his friend
and felt sure that the young elf
would now take steps to clean up
the house. But Hollyhock's next
words were the last ones he
expected to hear.

"In that case," said Hollyhock, "I'll leave the house and go to live in a tree."

Tumbledown rubbed his ears. Maybe that sneezing in the pepper mine *had* permanently affected them. But Hollyhock was speaking again, and even more firmly.

"Yes," he said, "that's exactly what I'll do. There's no nonsense about housework if you live in a tree, and everything smells nice *all* the time."

"But the cold … and the wind … and the rain!" cried Tumbledown, who liked to be comfortable.

"I shall make myself a little house," explained Hollyhock, "just big enough to keep me warm and dry, but *not* big enough to need furniture. And when it needs cleaning and dusting, I shall open the doors and windows and let the wind and the rain do the job for me. I don't know why I didn't think of it before. In fact, I don't know why *all* elves don't live in trees. I'm sure I've read that they used to in the old days."

Tumbledown had to admit that he had heard something similar himself, so perhaps it wasn't such a crazy idea after all.

"I'll come with you and help you to choose a suitable tree," he said. "That will be very important."

Several elves wondered why Hollyhock and Tumbledown were spending so much time walking up and down in Shady Wood. They were even more surprised when the two elves began to carry planks of wood into the trees.

"What on earth can he be doing?" asked Cowslip, as she finished her shopping one morning and almost bumped into Hollyhock, tottering along under the weight of a large mattress. "I thought my Mayflower was the silliest elf in town, but now I'm not so sure."

The very next day, her question was answered, when every elf in the town received an invitation.

This is what it said:

HOLLYHOCK ELF

invites you to his

TREEHOUSE WARMING

(four trees from the holly bush in Shady Wood)

PLEASE BRING A BOTTLE

OF SOMETHING NICE.

Well, there wasn't an elf in Elftown who wasn't eager to see exactly what had been happening in Shady Wood, especially when another notice appeared on Hollyhock's cottage, pinned to the middle of the front door.

> **Gone to live in Shady Wood.**
>
> **No deliveries here please.**

All the elves trooped into the wood, looking all around for signs of a little house among the trees. But at the foot of the fourth tree from the holly bush, they could see nothing at all.

"Yoohoo!" called a voice. "I'm up here, neighbours!"

And there was Hollyhock, peering out of a tiny little house, high up in the branches of the tree.

Cowslip asked what everyone was thinking. "But why?" she called. "What was wrong with your nice little house in town?"

"Let's just say," said Hollyhock, "that it had certain disadvantages. I don't want to say anything else about it. This cosy treehouse is much more my style."

Elves are good at giving parties, and the one that followed was remembered for a very long time. By the time the last elf wandered home, Hollyhock's new home was well and truly warmed.

That night, Hollyhock tucked himself up in his new bed and felt happier than he had been for a long time. He closed his eyes and drifted off to sleep to the sound of rustling leaves and the sighing of the wind.

Hollyhock was very tired that night, and he slept well. The next day, lots of his old friends came back to visit him. It was just like the old days, and Hollyhock enjoyed chatting and laughing with the other elves even more for being on his own so long.

But that night, the peaceful world of the treetops changed. The wind rose and, instead of sighing through the branches, it howled. Even the large branches, on which the treehouse was perched, began to sway. Hollyhock woke in the middle of the night feeling not seasick but treesick.

Then there were the little woodland noises that sound so pleasant during the day and so very worrying at night – little squeaks and squeals, some growls, and some snorting and snuffling.

437

By the morning, Hollyhock was a nervous wreck.

"*Anything* is better than this," he said to himself, climbing unsteadily down the tree. "There is only one thing to do."

And that is why the elves who passed his town house that day heard a lot of huffing and puffing inside and saw a new notice on the front door.

SPRING CLEANING
in progress.
Please visit tomorrow
(and every day after that!)

Sleepy
Snowdrop

You may have met many elves in your time, but I'm sure that you've never met one that was as sleepy as Snowdrop.

Everyone in Elftown knew that it was quite usual to come across Snowdrop lying peacefully asleep almost anywhere.

Cowslip once fell over her, sleeping in the sun outside the bakery. Twinkletoes sprayed her with water once when he was washing his wheelbarrow. She had crept inside and fallen fast asleep. It all became more than a joke when old Mrs Mallow nearly collapsed with fright when she opened her shed and saw a little face peering back at her. After all, no one expects to find a sleeping elf in her potting shed!

Some of the elves got together to decide what to do.

"I say that little elf is just lazy," grumbled Acorn. "You never heard of elves falling asleep during the day when *I* was young, I can tell you. It's a disgrace and must be stopped."

"Perhaps she's ill," said Cowslip. "Maybe she has a kind of sleeping illness and needs some medicine."

"Nonsense!" cried Acorn. "Old Doctor Driftwood from Goblinville had a look at her only the other

week, and he said that she was
perfectly fine. You know how wise
those goblin doctors are."

"I think she's under a spell,"
said Mayflower, who had recently
had quite a lot of trouble from
magic. "Maybe a wicked wizard
has enchanted her, so that she
can hardly keep her eyes open."

Everyone was a little quiet after
this. It certainly was something to
think about. But on the whole, it
seemed unlikely.

"There hasn't been a wizard
through here for at least a couple
of years," said Acorn, "and come
to think of it, Snowdrop was a
perfectly ordinary little elf then.

I still say she's lazy. Young elves today don't know what hard work is. When I was young…"

"Yes, yes," Cowslip broke in. Once he got started, Acorn could keep on all day about what happened when he was a boy. "The question is," Cowslip went on quickly, "what are we going to do? Things can't go on like this. Someone – probably Snowdrop herself – is going to get hurt."

"I think we should go and talk to her mother," suggested Twinkletoes. "She should really sort this out."

"But didn't you know?" asked Mayflower. "Her mother has been rather poorly for a long time now. I don't think we should worry her. We should try to solve the problem by ourselves."

"Someone should follow Snowdrop," said Acorn, "and see where she goes. Then at least we can stop her falling asleep somewhere dangerous. We can take turns."

So it was agreed. Twinkletoes waited outside Snowdrop's house the first morning until she came out. He followed her to the shops, where she bought some elf bread and a bag of apples. She put them in her basket and turned to visit the greengrocer's. Then, to

Twinkletoes' surprise, she fell asleep right in the middle of the road! Of course, the kindly elf woke her at once, before a goblin carriage ran her over. Then he helped her to pick up her apples, which had rolled all over the street and across the pavement.

After that, it wasn't much use following her further, because she knew perfectly well that poor Twinkletoes was there!

Next day it was Acorn's turn. The old elf couldn't move as quickly as Twinkletoes, but then Snowdrop walked along dragging her feet as well, so it didn't really matter. Acorn followed the sleepy girl out into the countryside, where she began to pick berries. But after only a few minutes, she sank down into a bramble bush and fell fast asleep.

Even Acorn couldn't help but feel sorry for her when he saw her poor scratched hands as he helped her out of the brambles.

On the third day, Mayflower followed Snowdrop down to the river, where she began to pick some flowers. But before very long, she sat down on the sunny bank and closed her eyes.

Luckily, Mayflower stayed watching for a while, because in a few minutes the little elf, still fast asleep, rolled down the bank and fell, with hardly a splash, into the deep, swirling water!

Mayflower may have been rather silly about some things, but he was a very good swimmer. Without a thought, he jumped into the fast-flowing water and swam strongly after the little elf, who had fallen on to a floating lily leaf and had not even woken as she was swept down the river.

Within a few minutes, Mayflower had pulled the dripping elf from the river.

"I'm going to take you home to Cowslip," he said kindly. "She will find us both some dry clothes and know what to do next."

When Cowslip saw the two soaking elves, she hurried them inside. After hot baths and a steaming mug of elf tea, they both felt better. And Cowslip told Mayflower that he had been an extremely brave elf and she was very proud of him indeed.

Then Cowslip turned to Snowdrop with a smile and said softly, "My dear, I think it is time that you and I went to see your mother. I think I know what is happening, and it is high time that it was sorted out. We will take this apple pie with us."

So Snowdrop and Cowslip walked slowly through Elftown, until they came to the tumbledown cottage where Snowdrop lived with her mother.

Inside, everything was neat and tidy. The furniture was polished and gleamed in the lamplight. There were flowers in the vases and piles of freshly ironed washing waiting to be put away. Snowdrop led the way upstairs, where, in a little bedroom that was as neat and tidy as any elf's room you have ever seen, a frail lady sat in a comfortable bed.

"How lovely to see you," she said to Cowslip. "I've often asked Snowdrop to bring her friends home, but she is always so busy. The doctor says that I shall be fine as long as I don't overdo it for a while. In the meantime, Snowdrop keeps the house looking beautiful. She cooks me lovely meals and does all the washing and ironing. I don't know how she finds time to do everything she does for me."

"I do," said Cowslip gently. "Little Snowdrop works half the

night to make everything nice for you. Then she falls asleep during the day because she is so tired. We are all very proud of her, but it is time that we made some better arrangement. How about this…" And Cowslip went on to explain what she had in mind.

Snowdrop's mother is better now, and Snowdrop has never again fallen asleep except in her own little bed. That's because every elf in Elftown helped her for a while. And who did the most? Old Acorn felt so badly about his harsh words that he spent all his time doing what he could … until *he* fell asleep in the cabbage patch!

The Goblin Gathering

Every so often, there is a great event in the lives of goblins everywhere. That is when the new goblin King is chosen. Then goblins from far and wide come together to make the choice. This event is called the Goblin Gathering, and if you ever get the chance to attend one, I recommend you to do so. It is not like any other gathering in all the fairy lands.

For one thing, goblins enjoy a good argument more than anything else in the world, except perhaps a toadstool stew and a cup of juniper juice, which would make anyone else very ill indeed but somehow seem to suit hardy goblin digestions.

But during a Goblin Gathering, juniper juice and toadstool stew are hardly thought of. The goblins are much more interested in arguing with each other about the good and bad points of all the candidates for the post of King.

In fact, this is such a sight to see that sometimes elves creep up and watch when they think that the goblins are so busy arguing they won't notice a ring of bright little eyes in the background. For elf Kings are born, not chosen.

At the time of this story, the old goblin King had just died, as goblin Kings do when they are very, very old. As you know, goblins live much longer than humans, sometimes as much as three hundred years.

Now a goblin King must be wise and kind. He must listen carefully to what goblins are saying and make sure that the old goblin ways are remembered. For goblins know a great deal that even elves have forgotten, such as how to make snowflakes and where to find the nest of the magic phoenix bird in the middle of the desert.

At this Gathering, there were three candidates for the post of King. The first was Griffin, a tall goblin with a long beard. He was said to have read every goblin book ever written, and that is a very big number indeed.

The second candidate was Borage, who knew more about goblin traditions than any other goblin. He could tell you when goblins first learnt to make thistledown and the names of all the goblin Kings from the beginning of time.

Last but by no means least was Burdock, the kindest goblin you ever met. Some people, especially elves, think that goblins are rather fierce and unfriendly, but Burdock was not like that at all. He went out of his way to be nice to everyone, and if you were in trouble, he was the first goblin you would turn to.

These goblins came to the forest to answer the Three Questions.

All the other goblins gathered round, anxious to hear their answers. By tradition, the oldest goblin of all asked the questions.

The first was a history question. "When," asked the oldest goblin, "did the Great King Tempest build the first goblin town?"

"It was in the third year of his reign," replied Griffin, who had read King Tempest's own book on the subject.

"No," said Borage, "what a foolish thing to say. It was in the fourth year of his reign. King Tempest himself made a mistake when he wrote his own book. Every historian knows that."

Burdock spoke last. "I don't know which of my friends here is correct," he said. "Does it really matter? Surely what we need to worry about is how well we build goblin towns today."

At that, all the goblins began to discuss the answers of the three candidates. Above the noise, a clear voice could be heard. It was Swallow, the daughter of the last King.

"Indeed, it is true that there was a mistake in King Tempest's book," she said, "but it was not he who made it. The scribe who copied out the King's notes found it hard to read his writing and made a small error. It was not his fault, and the fact has been put right in more recent versions of the book. We must always try to be fair about the past. Only then can we act well in the present and the future."

There was a small silence. The goblins had been given plenty to think about. Then the oldest goblin asked the second question.

"If the King's palace caught fire," he said, "and there was only time to save one thing from the flames, would you save a little goblin kitchen boy, hiding under a table, or the great Crown of Crowns with its gold and jewels?"

"That is not an easy question," replied Griffin. "Naturally, one would wish to save the boy, but the Crown of Crowns is unique. It can never be replaced, and it was the Great Wizard who first made it. We have a duty to save as much of our goblin history as we can. Regretfully, I would choose the Crown of Crowns."

"This time my rival is right," said Borage, "although his answer was expressed in such a long-winded way that I almost fell asleep. A King must often make hard choices. I do not shrink from that. The Crown of Crowns is of enormous importance in goblin history. It must be saved."

When Burdock spoke, his voice shook with emotion. "There is no question in my mind," he said. "The life of a single goblin is worth more than any crown. I would save the boy."

Once again, everyone spoke at once, but Swallow's voice again rose above them all.

"My friend Burdock is right," she said. "Every goblin is precious. But our history is important too. A question like this should not arise. If some little singing birds were allowed to fly through the palace night and day, in return for good food and a comfortable nest, they would warn us at the very first sign of a fire. Then it could be put out long before the crown or the boy were in danger."

One again there was a hush after she had spoken, before the oldest goblin asked his final question to the candidates.

"What is the most important thing you can see at this moment?" he asked, turning to look at the three goblins.

This time, it was Borage who spoke first. "The throne," he said simply, "which has been carried here from the royal palace. I hope to be seated upon it before the day is over."

Griffin gave a small smile and took from his robe a mirror of polished silver. Holding it up to his face, he said, "Myself! I am the goblin who will hold the future of all goblins in his hands. A King cannot afford false modesty. I am the most important thing that I can see."

"My friends," cried Burdock. "I am astonished at these answers, although I am sure they are well meant. The most important things that I can see are the faces of every goblin here and the love for our goblin people that I see shining out of them. That is what is truly important, and we should not forget it."

As the candidates finished their answers, the noise was deafening. But one or two goblins waited to hear what Swallow would say. Her calm voice seemed to still the gathering as she began to speak.

"I love our goblin people," she said, "but I see something without which no living thing could survive. Not a goblin, not a bird, not a flower, not a tree. It is the sunlight, sparkling through the branches. That is more important than all our words and deeds."

Now the arguments began in earnest. Each goblin had a favourite among the candidates. Voices rose and the talk was hot and fierce. The elves watching in the background hugged themselves with glee. Who would win this contest and rule the whole of the goblin kingdom?

Above the shouts of the crowd, a voice called for silence. To everyone's surprise, it was the oldest goblin who spoke.

"To my mind," he said solemnly, "one goblin alone has shown wisdom, learning and kindness today. That person should be our next ruler. Goblins, I beg you to greet in the time-honoured fashion, our first and only Queen … Swallow!"

In the space of a heartbeat, every goblin present knew that he was right, and a great cheer rose up among the branches. Another Goblin Gathering had come to its right and proper end.

How Petal
Found
a Home

It is a tradition among goblins that if another goblin asks for shelter, they should be given it. But sometimes things don't quite work out like that.

There was once a goblin called Petal. She worked as a cook in a large goblin home, where she was treated as one of the family. But gradually, the children left home to find work and homes of their own, and at last there was no more work for Petal to do, and she knew that she would have to leave.

"Don't worry," she told the mother of the family, "at least among goblins you are always sure of a bed for the night if you have no home to go to.

Petal set out to travel to the village where she was born. She knew that there would be goblins who still remembered her, and she hoped to find another home where she could cook and look after the family.

It was a long journey, but Petal found friendly faces wherever she went because she was a friendly goblin herself.

When she reached her own village, however, things were rather different. The first person she saw was old Mr Mumbles, who was digging in his garden.

"Hello, Mr Mumbles," called Petal. "Do you remember me? I used to live here, in the little cottage by the stream."

"You do look familiar, my dear," said Mr Mumbles, "although my eyes are not as good as they used to be. How can I help you?"

"I was hoping," said Petal, "that you would be able to have me to stay with you until I find a place of my own. I'll be no trouble and I can cook for you."

"Oh dear," said Mr Mumbles, "I'm afraid that won't do at all. My sister is staying with us at the moment, so we don't have a spare room. And anyway, I'm afraid my wife might not like another goblin in her kitchen."

"Never mind," said Petal cheerfully, "I'll ask someone else. Good afternoon, Mr Mumbles!"

Petal walked on into the village. It was a lovely, sunny day, and she soon came across Mulberry, hanging out rows and rows of washing.

"Hello, Mulberry! Do you remember me?" asked Petal, giving a friendly smile.

"Of course I do. It's Petal, isn't it?" cried Mulberry. "How lovely to see you again. Are you coming back to live with us?"

"Yes, indeed," said Petal. "And I was wondering if you would be able to have me to stay with you while I'm finding my feet. Would that be all right?"

"Oh, Petal," said Mulberry. "I do wish that I could help you. Since you went away, Mudlark and I have had three little boys, and there isn't an inch of space anywhere in our cottage. I am so sorry. Perhaps you could try Daisy down the road."

"I will," said Petal. "Goodbye!"

Daisy was not at home when Petal knocked on her door, but by chance Petal met her coming down the street with her shopping basket. The two goblins were very happy to see each other. They had grown up together and been in the same class at the goblin school.

"I'm so sorry I was out when you called," said Daisy, "but I had to get some things for supper. My whole house is being redecorated, and I can't use the kitchen at the moment, so I've bought some rolls instead."

"I suppose that means you don't have much room for a

visitor at the moment?" asked Petal, her heart sinking.

"My dear, I'm so sorry," said Daisy, "but you would be sleeping with your feet in a paint pot!"

Petal was beginning to feel that even that would be better than nothing, but she smiled cheerfully and went on her way.

Mrs Gooseberry was coming out of the bakery. "Why, if it isn't Petal!" she called in a friendly way. "What have you been doing with yourself? It must be years since you were back here. I hope you'll be staying this time. I'm afraid I can't stop. I'm rushing home to cook tea for some visitors and I've got just half an hour to do it in."

"But…" Petal began. She need not have bothered. Mrs Gooseberry was already halfway down the street.

Poor Petal was just beginning to think that she would have to lie down under a hedge that night, when she passed an empty shop. It was rather shabby, but Petal could see that it had once been a fine building.

"Do you know who owns this building?" Petal asked a passing goblin, for an idea had come into her mind. "If I can't stay with anybody and cook in their home," she said to herself, "I'll start my own restaurant. Everyone seems to be so busy and in such a hurry, I'm sure they'd like to come and eat out every once in a while. It would be a treat for everyone."

And that is just what happened. That very afternoon, Petal found the owner of the shop and persuaded her to let her move into the building. Then she rolled up her sleeves and set to work. Less than a week later, half the village was coming to eat at Petal's Parlour.

"I don't know what we did without you, my dear," said Mrs Mumbles. "My sister-in-law was always trying to help in the kitchen, and she's a terrible cook. I'm glad to get out and eat some delicious food again."

Everyone was glad that Petal had come back, and you can be sure that any stranger visiting the village will find a bed for the night at Petal's Parlour.